"THAT'S WHAT YOU FEEL SO GUILTY ABOUT—FEELING LIKE A SENSUAL, ENTICINGLY DESIRABLE WOMAN."

Laine shrank back. She couldn't deny his words as even now another shockwave of guilt flooded her. She'd let herself give in completely to Clay's kiss. Who was she kidding? And how could she have let herself go like that? She was so wrapped up in her own shame that for a moment she completely forgot that it was Clay, after all, who'd made the advance. When her rage surfaced, it helped her push those guilt feelings to the back of her mind.

"What you did was inexcusable!" The color had drained from her face. Her voice crackled with cold fury. "If you were trying to prove something, I guess you can feel proud of yourself. You're right. I do feel guilty. I don't like having my body betray me. But I am normal—despite what you may think. I can get aroused, excited, feel passion. I have needs, desires. . . ." She was shouting and crying at the same time. How dare he provoke her, unearth all of the passions she'd held so long at bay.

CANDLELIGHT ECSTASY ROMANCES®

218 STORMY SURRENDER, *Jessica Massey*
219 MOMENT TO MOMENT, *Bonnie Drake*
220 A CLASSIC LOVE, *Jo Calloway*
221 A NIGHT IN THE FOREST, *Alysse Rasmussen*
222 SEDUCTIVE ILLUSION, *Joanne Bremer*
223 MORNING'S PROMISE, *Emily Elliott*
224 PASSIONATE PURSUIT, *Eleanor Woods*
225 ONLY FOR LOVE, *Tira Lacy*
226 SPECIAL DELIVERY, *Elaine Raco Chase*
227 BUSINESS BEFORE PLEASURE, *Alison Tyler*
228 LOVING BRAND, *Emma Bennett*
229 THE PERFECT TOUCH, *Tate McKenna*
230 HEAVEN'S EMBRACE, *Sheila Paulos*
231 KISS AND TELL, *Paula Hamilton*
232 WHEN OPPOSITES ATTRACT, *Lois Walker*
233 TROUBLE IN PARADISE, *Antoinette Hale*
234 A BETTER FATE, *Prudence Martin*
235 BLUE RIDGE AUTUMN, *Natalie Stone*
236 BEGUILED BY A STRANGER, *Eleanor Woods*
237 LOVE, BID ME WELCOME, *JoAnna Brandon*
238 HEARTBEATS, *Jo Calloway*
239 OUT OF CONTROL, *Lori Copeland*
240 TAKING A CHANCE, *Anna Hudson*
241 HOURS TO CHERISH, *Heather Graham*
242 PRIVATE ACCOUNT, *Cathie Linz*
243 THE BEST THINGS IN LIFE, *Linda Vail*
244 SETTLING THE SCORE, *Norma Brader*
245 TOO GOOD TO BE TRUE, *Alison Tyler*
246 SECRETS FOR SHARING, *Carol Norris*
247 WORKING IT OUT, *Julia Howard*
248 STAR ATTRACTION, *Melanie Catley*
249 FOR BETTER OR WORSE, *Linda Randall Wisdom*
250 SUMMER WINE, *Alexis Hill Jordan*
251 NO LOVE LOST, *Eleanor Woods*
252 A MATTER OF JUDGMENT, *Emily Elliott*
253 GOLDEN VOWS, *Karen Whittenburg*
254 AN EXPERT'S ADVICE, *Joanne Bremer*
255 A RISK WORTH TAKING, *Jan Stuart*
256 GAME PLAN, *Sara Jennings*
257 WITH EACH PASSING HOUR, *Emma Bennett*

TENDER AWAKENING

Alison Tyler

A CANDLELIGHT ECSTASY ROMANCE®

Published by
Dell Publishing Co., Inc.
1 Dag Hammarskjold Plaza
New York, New York 10017

ISBN: 0-440-18647-1

Printed in the United States of America
First printing—August 1984

To Our Readers:

We have been delighted with your enthusiastic response to Candlelight Ecstasy Romances®, and we thank you for the interest you have shown in this exciting series.

In the upcoming months we will continue to present the distinctive, sensuous love stories you have come to expect only from Ecstasy. We look forward to bringing you many more books from your favorite authors and also the very finest work from new authors of contemporary romantic fiction.

As always, we are striving to present the unique, absorbing love stories that you enjoy most—books that are more than ordinary romance.

Your suggestions and comments are always welcome. Please write to us at the address below.

Sincerely,

The Editors
Candlelight Romances
1 Dag Hammarskjold Plaza
New York, New York 10017

CHAPTER ONE

Laine Sinclair sighed with relief as the taxi pulled up in front of her Georgetown apartment. All the way from the airport the driver had openly checked her out in the rearview mirror, forcing her to pretend avid interest in a route through Washington, D.C., that she knew like the back of her hand. His flirtatious though innocuous prattle was not difficult to tune out. She stifled a yawn out of politeness. The weariness she felt had little to do with the driver. It had been building for quite a while.

For the hundredth time she rehashed her last speech, trying to decide if she had given as effective a talk as she should have. Could she be getting stale after all this time? There was no doubt that these tours took a great deal out of her. Yet, her drive and determination had never wavered. Inwardly she was as fervent as ever. But outwardly . . .

How many similar speaking engagements had she made over the past few years? Different towns, different parts of the country, and different faces, but all connected by a single link—a concern for the men still listed as Missing In Action from the Vietnam War and the subsequent skirmishes in Cambodia. MIA. Those letters were as familiar to Laine as her own initials, indelibly printed in her mind since that warm spring day five years ago when she opened up the official letter from the Air Force informing her that her fiancé, James Lawrence, was missing in action in Cambodia.

Taking her small suitcase from the driver at the door to her brownstone, Laine smiled and thanked him. He beamed back at her, offering his services any time she needed a cab to the airport.

She felt a little guilty coming straight home instead of stopping back at the MIA headquarters. It was only 2:30 P.M. and as president of the Washington, D.C., branch of the organization, Laine knew her desk would be swamped after three days absence. When she had switched from a volunteer worker to a full-time paid employee of the organization she had not fully realized how enormously time-consuming and all-absorbing her job was going to be. She was certainly well paid for the hard work and grueling hours, but it was not the money that kept her going. It was her total dedication. But for once she opted to put her own needs first. A long soak in the tub and an early night was all she could think about during the flight from Massachusetts.

Part of her sluggish mood had to do with her disappointment about this particular speaking tour at the top New England colleges. Attendance had been uniformly low, and the students seemed indifferent to her organization's quest. Ruefully Laine acknowledged that for most undergraduates the war was long over and already a dead issue. She shivered despite the warm July afternoon.

Stepping into her hot, stuffy apartment, Laine caught her reflection in the hall mirror. Her thick mane of chestnut hair, always impossible to contain, now fell in a wild profusion of tousled waves around her small heart-shaped face. Laine had a fresh-scrubbed all-American type of beauty, with pale peach skin, huge, disarming brown eyes fringed with long, dark lashes, and, except for this afternoon, a nonstop vitality that often made people think she was a lot younger than her twenty-seven years. Until she spoke. Then her crisp, literate, knowledgeable style, coupled with a fierce passion, gave her an aura of maturity that stretched beyond her age.

Laine knew she was strikingly attractive, but over the past few years she had viewed her looks as more of a handicap than an asset. Every time she stood up in front of a group she was faced with the challenge of getting her audience to see beyond her appearance to the importance of what she was saying. Her success at public speaking had been gratifying—and it had kept her going.

She pulled her thin cotton blouse from her damp chest. It was stifling in the apartment. Flicking on the air conditioner, Laine stripped off the pale blue blouse and print skirt. As she slipped out of her low-heeled sandals she wriggled her toes, happy to be free of the uncomfortable bands of leather.

Tossing her lacy bra and panties on the edge of the bed in preparation for her bath, Laine stretched languidly, sinking down on the crisp sheets to relish the coolness that was finally filling the room. Objectively, she gazed down at her petite, slender form, acknowledging that she had a terrific body—full, firm breasts, a small waist, perfectly proportioned hips, and surprisingly long, shapely legs for someone so tiny. Jim always used to tease her that she was all legs. And then he would laugh in that deep, throaty way of his, and gazing at her enticingly he'd say, "Well, almost all."

She closed her eyes, lost in her fantasy. It was always the same. She'd be lying alone in bed and the door would spring open. First, all Laine would see was a thick crop of sandy-blond hair. Then Jim's smiling face would peek into the room. Laine would sit bolt upright and Jim would grin disarmingly and say, "You didn't think I'd stay away forever, did you, pigeon?"

Pigeon. He had bestowed that nickname on her shortly after they'd begun dating in their sophomore year of college. Laine used to collect leftover bread from her meals in the dorm and stroll through the park, feeding the birds. When Jim went along with her one day, he complained that the only birds who seemed to get the goodies were the greedy pigeons. Laine argued that she admired the pigeons most of all. They were bold, determined survivors who went after what they wanted rather than hanging back waiting for a morsel to land by chance in their beaks. Laughing at her intensity, Jim affectionately dubbed her Pigeon and the nickname had come to prove accurate. Laine, too, had learned to be a determined survivor.

In her fantasy, Jim would walk slowly up to her, his eyes sparkling. Laine always lifted the covers, welcoming him home at last. She could feel his lean, taut nakedness against her flesh, their mutual heat engulfing them in flames of desire. Once again, he would tenderly caress her yearning body in all the ways she loved, fanning her passion and need. She'd cling to him, whispering her love and her infinite joy at his return, begging him never to leave her again. And he would kiss the rosy tip of each of her breasts in a solemn vow to stay there with her always.

The jarring, shrill ring of the telephone startled Laine out of her daydream. She made no move to pick up the receiver, as the phone was still connected to her answering machine, but she sat up, angry with herself. These visions inevitably led to an upsetting frustration. Over the past year especially, she had made a concerted effort to control her fantasies about Jim. For the most part she had been successful, learning in the process to relax more. She had begun to force herself to socialize, to stop using her work as an excuse not to have a social life.

Through her involvement with the MIA group she had cultivated many close relationships. As long as she kept her social involvements casual she could handle them. Those first couple of years that Jim was missing, Laine had attacks of guilt whenever she had any fun. Lately she had come to accept the fact that perpetual mourning helped no one. She was more realistic these days. She was beginning to laugh more, enjoy more activities, feel more confident about her ability to cope without Jim. Except when her fantasies surfaced full-force like today.

After a few minutes Laine listened to her answering machine. A half-dozen messages, mostly from the office, and then the last one from Clay Marsh. Clay worked for the Undersecretary for Special Affairs and for the past three years he had acted as the liaison between the MIA group and the Pentagon. He was an invaluable ally as well as a dear friend. She and Clay had shared some joyous moments in their work together and a great many sad ones, the bond between them growing with each occasion. At Laine's most despairing times Clay had been there for her, supporting, bolstering, caring. She often wondered what she would have done without him these last few years as her hopes for Jim became dimmer and dimmer.

Peoples' voices always sounded a little awkward and strained on the tape, but Laine had heard Clay's voice dozens of times on her machine. She knew immediately from his tone that something was wrong. Suddenly clammy and chilled, Laine flicked off the air conditioner. In his message Clay had asked Laine to come down to his office this afternoon if she got home in time. Otherwise he would stop by her house after work.

Taking a quick shower, Laine tried to get a grip on herself. Why was she feeling so panicked that the news was about Jim? Clay always called her first if he got word—good or bad—about any of the MIAs. If the information involved someone Laine knew personally, she would be the bearer of the happy or sad tidings. Mostly the news was bad, and it was not a job Laine relished. But she accepted it along with the rest of the responsibilities she had assumed when she had dedicated herself to this work.

She hurriedly dressed in a flower-print shirtwaist dress with a warm yellow background. The color was a conscious choice. It was cheerful and bright, and she was determined not to allow her bleak mood to surface. After a quick call to tell Clay's secretary that she was on her way, Laine reached over to her end table for her purse.

A snapshot of her and Jim set in a simple gold

frame fell over as Laine grabbed her pocketbook. She retrieved it, gently setting it back on the table. She looked at the smiling couple captured on film. It had been taken at their engagement party five years ago, just days before Jim left for Vietnam. Laine studied the picture closely. They were embracing, half laughing, half kissing, Jim lifting her off the ground in the process. They looked so young, so deliriously happy. When he'd gotten his orders to go overseas, Laine had been terrified, but he'd held her in his arms reassuringly, telling her that their love was stronger than any war and they had too many beautiful plans for him not to return. Besides, as a general's aide, he'd be well out of the line of fire. Laine, wanting to believe their love would protect him, put her fears aside. He would come back to her. She'd felt it with a certainty that had taken years to diminish.

Now, as she ran her fingers gently over the snapshot of Jim's lean form, tears streamed down her face. So handsome and full of ambition. Their love had been so perfect, the years ahead of them promising such happiness. And this was all she had to nurture her—a slightly faded photo giving only a hint of the man himself and of the beautiful love they had shared. Tenderly she brought the photo to her lips and kissed Jim. She could not shake her sense of finality about the gesture.

Clay must have been watching for Laine from his window. He was waiting in the outer office as she stepped in the door. He looked elegantly handsome, wearing, as always, an impeccably tailored business suit, this one a soft tan. Many times Laine had been struck by Clay's dark, fierce good looks. Not handsome by traditional standards, his face was rich with character. There was power, strength, and raw masculinity in his ruggedly etched features. His tall, well-muscled build added to the strong yet sensual appearance, as did his dark brown, almost black hair tinged with a distinguished bit of gray at the temples.

In their years working together Laine had come to learn that Clay was an extremely mercurial man. He could be totally captivating one moment, using his sharp wit and considerable charm to make things happen, and at other times his fiery temper could well up and boil over, searing whoever might be in his way. Laine had seen both these sides of him often over the years as they worked together struggling with the bureaucratic structure to try to get information and necessary action taken. With Laine, however, Clay had always been consistently warm and supportive. She knew they shared a unique and complex relationship and that their feelings for each other ran deep. Sometimes Laine lovingly called him Brother, but Clay always wore a strangely sad expression when she did. And on those few occasions when he held her to him and she experienced a rush of feelings that were far from sisterly, she quickly denied them.

It was not as easy to ignore Clay's attraction to her. She knew that she had only to give him the slightest encouragement for Clay to try to change their relationship into something more serious. But there was only one man in her life, and she had been straight with Clay from the start. Even though the possibility dwindled daily, she still held on to a fragment of hope that Jim would be found. Up to now Clay had accepted the holding position she was bound up in and he never pushed her. It had allowed Laine to maintain a special connection with Clay without feeling threatened.

As Laine crossed the room she concentrated her attention on Clay's face. Having been through so much together, she had learned to understand the deeper meanings behind his facial set. His compelling expression made her gasp. The look reflected a pained mixture of harshness and tenderness. It nearly undid her—her fears materializing into reality. Jim was dead. Clay didn't have to say a word.

As her step faltered Clay quickly rushed to her side. Putting a firm arm around her for support, he brought her into his office. Laine's body felt suddenly frozen, the icy feeling traveling up to her brain. For a few moments all thought ceased. And then slowly she began to recognize sensations. Clay's large but infinitely gentle hand caressed her back and shoulders.

"Tell me." Her voice was a bare whisper.

"The word came in from Cambodia this morning. A group of . . . of bodies . . . were uncovered in an old prisoner-of-war camp. The men are being identified slowly. The typical bureaucratic bullshit. We got two names today. A Paul Richardson from Detroit"—Clay took her hand—"and Jim Lawrence. Of course the Pentagon has ordered full military honors at Arlington for each of the men."

"Yes, of course." For a split second Laine imagined they were talking as they had many times before about men she had never known—strangers for whom she nevertheless felt a strong sadness and loss. But then the truth hit her with such force she doubled over in pain, a low, mournful wail escaping her throat.

"Oh, Jim, my darling, sweet Jim," she cried softly. Clay let her be for a few moments. This grief was hers alone. Then he gently but firmly put his arm around her and led her over to the brown leather couch across the room. She continued to cry as he pressed her to him.

"Okay, baby," he murmured. "Let it out. It's all right." He gently caressed her back, his lips placed lightly against her silken hair.

"It's strange," she said when the tears finally subsided and she lifted her head from Clay's shoulder. "I've prepared myself for this moment a thousand times. No matter how much I tried to believe some miracle would occur, I knew. I knew," she echoed in a whisper.

"You are better off knowing, Laine. Now you can finally put those fantasies and dreams of miracles to rest. You can bury him and start living again." Clay's voice was tender but firm.

He knew how shaken she was. She needed support to absorb the reality.

Sadly, she looked across at Clay. "I've buried him so many times in my mind. Why is it so hard this time?"

Clay turned her to him and took hold of her shoulders. "I know how tough this is for you. Believe me, honey, if I could ease the pain, I would. But at least all the waiting is over." As she tried to look away he cupped her chin. Clay wanted her to hear what he was telling her. He had watched her bury herself for too long. He let himself admit just how angry it had made him to see her always throwing aside her own needs. And his too. Again, he emphasized, "It's over."

"Is it?" she asked, still dazed. "I can't imagine it ever being really over."

"Right now you can't. But you will get through this. I intend to make sure that you do. You're too vibrant and alive, with too much to offer to keep yourself hidden away."

There was something in Clay's tone that made Laine look up sharply. His gaze was intense, his dark eyes conveying a message that Laine found disturbing, even a little frightening. There was a fierce determination in his manner. She was familiar enough with this side of his personality, but never when it came to her. It was as though he were letting her know that things were going to be different between them from now on.

Just as Laine was becoming more agitated, Clay abruptly switched moods.

"When did you eat last?" All at once he was back to being the warm, concerned friend he had always been. His tender scowl brought a vague smile to Laine's lips.

"I think I must have had breakfast this morning. To be honest, it was such a hectic day I can't really remember whether I ate or not."

Sweeping his arm around Laine, Clay said, "I'm going to buy you some dinner, young lady. Let's go."

"I—I can't even think about eating, not now. I know you're trying to help, Clay. But I need some time to be alone. I need to sort it out. Will I ever make any sense out of it all? Jim was so very much alive, so full of energy, so . . . so very young." She stepped away from Clay and turned her back.

Clay walked over to her and turned her around to face him. His scowl was far from tender now. "Damn it, Laine. You knew this was coming. You said so yourself. Let him go. Jim's dead. Do you hear me, Laine?" he shouted, shaking her more forcefully than he meant to. "I've stood by watching you grieve for a long time. I'm not going to watch you go on like that forever." His anger sprang up from a deep part of him. He had seen so much grief in this job—so many families faced with finally having to bury their loved ones after all the years of waiting. Some of the strongest had folded. He was not about to let this happen to Laine. She could not be allowed to seal herself up in memories, afraid to give, afraid to love. This time he cared too much.

"You can't understand, Clay. It isn't an issue of choice. He's inside of me. I don't know how to let him go," she cried out in anger and frustration.

"Then let me help you. Don't keep pushing me away. Don't keep trying to run away from your own feelings. You know what I'm talking about," he said with a fierce authority.

Laine was caught off-guard. "Clay, I don't understand why you're doing this to me."

"What am I doing, Laine? Being honest? We've been together for a long time. I know you very well."

Laine felt a desperate need to get away. Clay's penetrating eyes seemed to see things inside of her that she was not ready to face. She felt angry and betrayed. She had expected tenderness and compassion from Clay, not harsh realities and distressing innuendos. Pulling herself together, she hurried to the door. She felt far too vulnerable to engage in battle with Clay. All she wanted to do was get away.

Clay's voice stopped her as she caught hold of the brass knob.

"I'll drive you home." His voice was softer, gentler.

Laine kept her hand on the knob, looking at him over her shoulder. "I'm not running away. I just need some time. Please, Clay, I want to go home alone." Her voice had softened too. There was no missing the caring look in Clay's eyes.

She could see that he had not intended to be cruel. He was only trying to make her come to grips with Jim's death, to make her see that her grief had to have an end. The only problem was that she wasn't sure how to achieve that end.

When she murmured a quick good-bye and left, Clay didn't try to stop her. As he watched the door shut, he took a deep breath, trying to get his own emotions under control. Jim's death had opened a floodgate of feelings for him, too, feelings he'd been carefully keeping under wraps for some time. He glanced down at his hands. They were trembling. He shoved them into his pockets, cursing silently.

CHAPTER TWO

Laine walked the last few blocks to her apartment. Her body ached as though it had just been through a strenuous workout. But it was her mind and heart that had suffered the painful ordeal; her body merely reflected the trauma.

As she stepped into her apartment she felt stunningly alone. Wearily she dropped into the brown corduroy love seat, letting her head fall back on the cushions. She would have to call Jim's father. Ted Lawrence had long ago given up hope about his son. His way of coping with the loss had been to declare Jim dead years ago. Laine understood, even though it saddened her to know his father had placed Jim in a small pocket of his mind. Ted had remarried last year, and Laine rarely had any contact with him. But she knew he had somehow managed to bury the past and go on with his own life.

Over the years she had dealt with so many families of MIA soldiers, learning in the process that there were many ways of grieving and coping with the loss. Some people grew bitter and hard, others strove to put the past aside and deny the pain of the loss. And then there were those people, like herself, who captured the memory and held on to it for dear life.

Laine did not think her way was best. She knew her tight hold on the past kept her isolated. Lately she had been making a concerted effort to get out more, to control her daydreams, to stop believing that a miracle was going to occur. But the one thing she couldn't shake was the special sense of emptiness Jim's disappearance had created. In her dreams especially, Jim's memory haunted her. She always held a part of herself in reserve—a part that belonged to Jim. For all her intellectualizing, she had still held on to her hope. And now that hope had been irrevocably destroyed.

Had their relationship not been so ideal, maybe she would have been able to cope more easily. But invariably she found herself comparing other men to Jim and they always suffered from the comparison. Only with Clay had Laine been able to hold the comparisons at bay. While the two men were unique, they shared some wonderful qualities in common. Both Jim and Clay were genuine and honest about their emotions, never concerning themselves with image and posture. Neither of them needed to act macho—they were totally at ease being real people, not requiring a pseudo-strong image.

Clay was far more intense than Jim, his style and demeanor more serious. Jim was playful; he loved to pull harmless pranks. And he was a tease in a charming, ingenuous way. But then he had been so young. For a brief moment she tried to imagine what Clay might have been like at that age. Clay was thirty-four now, ten years older than Jim had been when he left her. A lot of changes could take place in ten years. A hollow emptiness engulfed her as she tried to figure out what her own life would be like ten years from now.

Again the loneliness weighed down on her with oppressive force. Why did it feel so much worse now? she wondered. Nothing had really changed, she rationalized. She'd been alone for years now, and certainly for the past couple of years she had begun to resign herself, on some level, to Jim's death. Still, the finality of it made the picture of her existence more vivid. Suddenly the energy that had driven her all these years seemed to evaporate.

With her defenses down, she began to think again about her meeting with Clay today. He had seemed so different. There was an intensity not only in the things he had said to her but in his manner. Once more she felt that same fear that she had experienced in his office. She had a strange sensation of slipping into danger. Always in the past she had felt so safe with Clay.

But now, thinking of him stirred up a growing apprehension.

She shut her eyes in an attempt to drive those thoughts of Clay from her mind. She had all she could handle at the moment. As soon as her lids closed, the phone rang. She wished she had remembered to switch on her answering machine, but in her haste to get to Clay's office she had forgotten all about it.

"Hello," she said wearily.

"How are you doing?"

Laine immediately recognized her secretary's voice. Carrie Miller was far more than Laine's employee; she was a dear friend. Only a year ago Laine had shared Carrie's grief when the news came of her husband's verified death in Vietnam.

"Not great," Laine admitted wryly. "I feel so unbelievably drained."

"It's a real bitch," Carrie agreed gently. "You wait all these years to hear something you already know but need to have confirmed because the uncertainty is so unbearable. Then the certainty comes and it's somehow no more tolerable. It gets easier, but you probably won't believe that any more than I did."

"You're right, but thanks." Laine sighed.

"Do you want some company?"

"Not tonight. After I call Jim's dad, I'm going to take the long bath I promised myself earlier this afternoon, then I'm going to try to get some sleep."

"Okay, but just remember that you've got a

lot of friends out there who understand what you're going through, and unfortunately too many of us who have gone through it ourselves. When you lose someone you love, it's important to know that you've got people out there who love you."

Laine didn't bother to wipe away the tears that were slipping down her cheeks. "I know. I'm going to need you all."

Almost as soon as Laine hung up the phone it rang again. Another friend from the office called to offer her condolences. Word traveled fast in their tight-knit organization. The phone would be ringing all evening.

Hanging up the receiver for the third time, she almost switched on the answering machine. She wanted to for her own peace of mind, craving the solitude right now far more than the condolences, but she understood that her friends needed the contact for themselves almost as much as for her. There was a strong bond between them born of their shared plight. In times of crisis it was important to reach out and connect.

Four phone calls later and no time for her promised bath, Laine was beginning to come unglued. When the phone and doorbell rang simultaneously, she almost screamed out loud. Opening her front door, she looked with relief into Clay's eyes.

Putting her hands to her ears, she said pleadingly, "Please answer the phone and tell whoever it is that I'm out or sleeping or anything. And tell them to stop calling." She was near hysterics.

Clay set the grocery bag he was carrying on the hall table and went to the phone.

"Pete, it's Clay." He paused for a moment to listen and then said, "She needs a little peace and quiet more than anything right now. Do me a favor, Pete, and spread the word to hold off on the calls for tonight. I'm going to stay with Laine and see that she gets some food into her and goes to bed. I think by tomorrow she'll be ready to talk with friends." Again he paused. "We appreciate it. Tell the others as well. It's going to be invaluable to her in the days ahead."

Something about the way Clay had said "We appreciate it" gave Laine a comforting feeling. He would see this through with her. It was a relief not to be feeling so alone. With Clay she could be herself. If she needed to collapse and fall apart, she was confident he would stand by and help her pick up the pieces afterward. She smiled warmly at him as he hung up the phone.

"You're a regular knight in shining armor," she said, her lips curving in a half smile. "I'm glad you decided to come by tonight."

He smiled back and walked over to the hallway to retrieve his bundle.

"At your service, beautiful damsel," he said as he bowed slightly, returning to her side. "But first things first. This knight's stomach is about to cave in from starvation, so come help me unload the groceries and turn on your stove." He stretched his hand out for her.

She knew he was purposely forcing her to occupy herself with something completely mundane. He knew she understood his motives. That it was obvious wasn't the point. It was exactly what she needed. Laine stood up and walked hand in hand with him into the kitchen.

Unloading the bundle, he took out a carton of eggs, a small plastic bag of exquisite-looking white mushrooms, and a brick of cheddar cheese. After Laine dug out her omelet pan from the cupboard and set it on the stove, Clay tossed her the bag of mushrooms.

"Slice them nice and thin," he ordered with a grin. "I hate large chunks of mushrooms in my omelets."

"Definitely crude," Laine agreed with a laugh, and then she put all her attention to her task. They worked together quietly and efficiently in Laine's small, cozy kitchen, getting the omelets, a salad of red leaf lettuce and avocado slices, and steaming mugs of tea, to the table. Settling down, they ate in comfortable silence.

"I was hungry," Laine said with astonishment as she regarded her empty plate.

"Most people who don't eat for ten or twelve hours usually are." He grinned at her across the table. "Now, do you want to wash or dry?"

Laine looked back at him with a smile. "Clay, how do you always manage to say just the right thing?"

They both laughed, understanding full well what Laine had meant. Clay had lifted Laine out of her depressed mood simply by keeping her busy with mindless little tasks. She was unendingly grateful.

"You know what I'd love more than anything at this moment?" she asked him.

"What's that?"

"I'd love to take a bath. A steamy, hot bubble bath."

"If this is your way of getting me to wash *and* dry the dishes . . ." he teased, smiling at her. "Okay, go soak, but next time you carry half the load."

"Forget the dishes." Laine laughed. "Why don't you go on home and get some rest? I'm fine now—really."

"I'll stay for a while longer. Go take your bath." His tone left no room for argument. Laine found herself glad that he hadn't followed her suggestion, because his presence did help a great deal. Despite her pronouncement of being okay, the truth was she felt relieved not to be left alone with her thoughts.

She managed to let her mind go blank as her body slowly relaxed in the soothing hot water. She could faintly hear that Clay had found some soft jazz station on the radio. The rhythmic music helped her unwind. The water finally cooled down so much that Laine forced herself to get out of the tub. Toweling off vigorously, she slipped on her terry robe and walked back into the living room.

"That bath must have had magic bubbles," Clay said, smiling as he sat on the couch. "You look a hell of a lot better. Here"—he patted the cushion next to him—"come sit down."

Laine sat beside Clay. "I feel better." The instant she said the words, her face paled, a frown streaking her brow. "Oh, no." It was more a sigh than an exclamation.

"What is it?" Clay's voice was immediately filled with concern.

"Jim's father. I—I've got to call him. I keep putting it off. Calling him makes it sound so—so final." She bent her head, her fingers tangling in her still damp curls.

Clay rubbed her back gently. In a soft tone he said, "Laine, it *is* final. There's no escaping the reality. No more dreams or fantasies or false hopes."

Laine's large brown eyes, filled with sorrow and tinged with hurt, shot up at him. Before she could say anything, he lifted a lock of her wayward hair and tenderly drew it away from her eyes. "I'm not trying to hurt you. And I'm not being callous. But the sooner you start believing the truth, the sooner you'll be able to pull yourself together. So go call Mr. Lawrence. I'll hang around."

Laine squeezed Clay's hand, feeling the comforting strength of his responsive grasp. She felt a stirring of a great many emotions as she sat next to this man who seemed to understand her better than she understood herself. With a slight quiver in her voice she said with resignation, "Okay. I'll make the call."

He watched her walk into her bedroom. She

was a petite, delicately beautiful young woman whose courage and caring had touched him for so long now. He had meant it when he told her he'd do anything to protect her, but he also knew that Laine's fragile looks and demeanor camouflaged a strong, vital, determined woman. It was time for her to face life once again, and Clay was going to do everything in his power to help her.

She returned a few minutes later looking more thoughtful than upset.

"How did it go?"

"Ted was naturally very sad, but he's quite a man. He said that he had been expecting the news. He told me he would always cherish the years he had with Jim." Laine hesitated. When she continued, her voice was a little shaky. "He said something else to me." Her eyes met Clay's. "He cautioned me not to turn Jim into some kind of a saint, not to hold him up as some perfect being that no one else could ever equal. He practically ordered me not to turn my back on life." Tears filled her eyes, a sad smile curving her lips. "Jim's dad is a hell of a lot stronger than me. Somehow he's managed to hold on to his love for his son and yet go on and find happiness. He's married again, has a daughter and even two stepsons with his new wife. I feel jealous. Isn't that awful?" She searched Clay's face for confirmation, and at first she misread his scowl.

"Laine, don't look to me to support your guilt feelings. You seem to do a good enough job of that on your own. In fact, over the years I think you've become very adept at using guilt to do just what Jim's father warned you about—turning your back on life."

Laine stared at him in outraged disbelief. "That's a lousy thing to say! Is that what you believe—that my life is guided by guilt?" Her eyes flashed with angry sparks. She didn't wait for an answer. "Well, since you think you know me so damn well, Mr. Marsh, just what am I supposed to be feeling so all-fired guilty about?" she asked heatedly, her words filled with challenge.

Clay knew how angry Laine felt at his accusation, but he couldn't help smiling as he saw the fiery sparkle in her glittering eyes. It was the first real sense of life he'd seen in her today.

Clay's smile only made Laine madder. She positively glowered at him, unaware that in her anger she had edged closer to him. Clay, however, was very aware of her nearness. He could almost feel the heat of her body. Her fragrant, soapy scent was intoxicating.

Suddenly he was grabbing her roughly to him, pressing her tightly against his powerful chest, his mouth capturing her lips. At first Laine was so astonished, she simply allowed the kiss, her body offering no resistance. But as his tongue searched hers out, the full impact of what was happening hit her. Struggling to free herself, her body merely pushed harder against Clay, who held her to him in an unyielding embrace. Something seemed to explode inside of them. A fire, astounding in its intensity, gripped them both. Hungrily they kissed more deeply, Laine's tongue reaching into the soft, warm recesses of Clay's mouth. She was oblivious of the fact that her robe was slipping open, the tie hanging loosely at her sides. She moaned as his hands slid under the robe, traveling in caressing waves across her supple, bare back. His touches were driving her on to an insane abandon. But she couldn't stop. The years of pent-up desire and need erupted inside of her as Clay kissed her passionately.

It was only when Clay began to ease the robe off her shoulders that Laine came back to her senses with riveting intensity, her cry of anguish so shrill that Clay immediately let go of her. Breathlessly she stared at him.

Clay's face was impossible to read as he gazed back at her. In a voice oddly calm after such an intense experience, he said, "That's what you feel so guilty about—feeling like a woman, a sensual, enticingly desirable woman."

Laine shrank back. She could not deny his words as even now another shock wave of guilt flooded her. She had let herself give in completely to Clay's kiss. Whom was she kidding? She had returned his kiss with equal fervor, letting herself become totally lost in the erotic sensations that were coursing through her. How could she have let herself go like that? She was so wrapped up in her own shame that for a moment she completely forgot about the fact that it was Clay, after all, who had made the advance.

When her rage at him surfaced, it helped her push those guilt feelings to the back of her mind.

"What you did was inexcusable." The color had drained from her face, and her voice crackled with a cold fury. "If you were trying to prove something, I guess you can feel proud of yourself. You're right. I do feel guilty. I don't particularly like having my body betray me. But I am normal, despite what you may think. I can get aroused, excited, feel passion. I have needs, desires. . . ." She was shouting and crying at the same time. How dare he provoke her, unearth all the passion she had held at bay for so long.

"Oh, God, Clay, why are you doing this to me?" She thought of all the experiences they had shared, the joys and sorrows they had weathered together, the friendship and trust that had come so naturally to them. Everything that had previously existed was suddenly out of focus, distorted by the heat and remnants of passion that still engulfed her.

Clay reached out to her, but when she shivered at his touch he let his hand fall to his side. He, too, felt shaken and unnerved. He wanted her—he wanted her desperately. Holding her in his arms, feeling her passionate response, he knew beyond a doubt that he had to have her.

"I'm in love with you, Laine. That kiss—it shook me as much as it did you. I've wanted to kiss you so damn many times. But Jim was always there in the shadows. There were times when I held you in my arms to comfort you and I wanted to force his image from your mind, make you realize that I could give you what you really longed for and needed. But I always stopped myself. Maybe the truth is I was having my own battle with guilty feelings. How could I try to win you away from a man who wasn't there to do his own fighting? Jim had a hold on you that I couldn't touch. Believe me, there were a lot of times I cursed my own sense of honor." He bent his head for a moment, raking his long fingers through his hair. When he looked up at her again, his face was tinged with bitterness.

"Jim has no hold on you anymore. You can stop struggling to fend off your own needs and desires. You can let yourself feel like a real woman again." His dark eyes studied her intimately, knowingly. "Laine, don't tell me there haven't been times you wanted me. I've watched you try to hide your yearning from yourself as much as from me. Look at me," he commanded huskily. "Until now, there was never a chance for us. I had to respect the fact that you had a commitment to Jim. Maybe if he had returned I could have fought him fair and square for you. Now I see it's you that I am going to have to fight. Feeling like a real woman obviously terrifies you."

"A real woman." She laughed bitterly. "You're damn right I'm scared! Maybe you think I should be eager to let myself fall in love again. Why? So I can risk going through all of this misery once more? I think I almost hate you at this moment. Hate you for stirring up feelings I don't want to feel." Her cold rage gave way to a painful ache. She cast him a helpless look. "I don't want you to love me, Clay. I don't want to let myself love you. I can't go through this all over again."

"Why are you so convinced loving has to lead to pain?" he demanded, snatching hold of her hand as she tried to bring it to her face to shield her tears.

"Why shouldn't I be convinced?" Her tears instantly stopped as she turned to confront him. "How many times since I've known you have you gone off on secret undercover missions, risking your life behind enemy lines to search for clues, to try to find out anything you could about the MIAs? Don't you know how often I found myself praying you'd come back safely, praying that you wouldn't be captured or killed yourself, like . . . like Jim and all the others? Can you imagine what it would be like for me if I were to let myself love you? No!" she screamed out. "No, I won't let myself go through another nightmare. Never. Do you hear me? Never."

She sprang out of her seat and raced into her bedroom. Clay could hear her sobs through the closed door.

For a few moments Clay remained where he was, his head sunk into his open palms. He sighed deeply, then slowly stood up and walked over to the bedroom door. He turned the handle, thankful that she hadn't locked herself inside. But when he stepped into the room, viewing her fragile form huddled on the large bed, clutching the panda bear Jim had given her, he realized that she was in fact locked inside herself—and that barrier was harder to break through than any door.

Clay sat down beside her on the edge of the bed. Her wide-eyed despairing look both pained and angered him. Touched only moments before by the unbelievably tempestuous side of her, he fought for compassion and control while his body still yearned for her.

For a brief while neither of them spoke. Laine finally lifted her eyes to meet Clay's gaze. She studied him carefully, a resigned expression replacing her sadness. Clay found this new look more disturbing, and her words only added to his upset.

"Clay, it will never work for us. I don't want to . . ."

"To what? To admit, possibly, feelings that already exist. There has been something between us for a long time now. Let's stop pretending." He sounded exhausted as he spoke.

Laine stretched her hand out and placed it over his. "Maybe that's true. I know I do care about you, Clay. But I can't handle another involvement. Maybe a part of me died along with Jim. I only know you deserve more than I can give. You should have a woman who can freely and fully give you all of her love, without restraint or fear. Can't you see that I'm not that woman?"

Clay could feel his anger mounting. He fought to contain the feeling, but it was useless. Maybe she was able to convince herself that she couldn't love again, but she damn well wasn't about to convince him.

"I'll tell you what I see. I see a frightened woman desperately trying to deny a basic part of herself. Nothing has died inside of you, Laine. Maybe you wish it had. But just that brief glimpse of your passionate nature tells me you're very much alive."

Laine turned away. Why wouldn't he leave her alone? Why did he have to keep tearing away at her defenses? But Clay was far from ready to let go. With biting harshness he snarled, "So what's the future going to be? Will you crawl into bed each night with that sad excuse for a companion?" he said, pulling the panda out of her arms and tossing it off the bed. "Or do you want a flesh and blood person who can excite your desires, fill you with his passion, love you the way you should be loved?" Once more he grabbed her up in his arms, but then, just as heatedly, he let go, causing her to tumble back onto the pillows.

"When you make up your mind, let me know," he said, turning away from her. He felt drained as he stood up and walked to the door.

"Clay."

He turned back to her, his hand resting on the doorknob.

"I hate what's happening. I don't want to see what we've had together destroyed." Her eyes looked pleadingly at him.

"Neither do I. I want to build on it. I want it

to be a foundation for something deeper." He opened the door and walked out, gently shutting the door after him.

Laine sank wearily against the pillows, Clay's words playing over in her mind. Was she a coward? Could she ever let herself love again? Tonight she had revealed a part of herself that she had spent years burying. Her physical needs had betrayed her. Only Clay, she knew, could have unleashed that part of her. Being honest with herself, she admitted that she always had been quick to fight off the feelings of longing he evoked in her body. She was ashamed of their very existence, her mind chastising her for her weakness. She had promised Jim her heart and soul.

The phone conversation with Jim's dad flashed in Laine's mind. He, too, loved Jim deeply. Yet, he had been able to put that love into perspective and not let it keep him from rediscovering happiness and fulfillment. Why couldn't it be the same for her? She knew it would be very easy to love a man like Clay. Even thinking of the possibility brought forth another rush of guilt. The image of Jim's handsome, smiling face filled with his love for her kept reappearing. And just as quickly she felt the sheer devastating pain of the loss. "No," she cried out, "never again."

Laine had no idea how she finally fell asleep, but as the sun streamed through the window she opened her eyes and found her arms entwined around her black panda. In her sleep she must have reclaimed him from the carpet where Clay had thrown him. She'd made her choice after all. Squeezing the bear with a wistful sigh, she placed him lovingly against the pillow beside hers and got out of bed.

CHAPTER THREE

The summer rainstorm darkened the morning, fitting in perfectly with the bleak moods of the group gathered together at Arlington Cemetery to bid their final farewells to Jim Lawrence. The military funeral was filled with pomp and ceremony. To Laine, the formal ritual cast a surrealistic aura over the proceedings. She felt oddly removed, as though she were going through motions that had little meaning. In her mind she had already held her own private burial for Jim and this affair was really for all the others—Jim's friends and family, and hers.

Laine's mother had taken time out from her busy schedule to attend the funeral. Her mother had become a social butterfly since her father's death five years ago. Roger Sinclair had become successful in real estate a few years before his death, and had left his wife and daughter financially secure for life. Laine rarely touched the trust fund he had left her; the earnings she made from being one of the few paid employees of the MIA organization met her needs quite adequately. Unlike her mother, Laine had never longed for expensive material possessions or a fast-paced social whirl of activity. Though Laine and her mother were totally different personalities with interests that were worlds apart, they shared a natural affection for each other. Holding her mother's hand was a comfort during the funeral service.

Clay maintained a close eye on Laine, but kept his distance. She knew he was concerned about how she would cope with the event and she smiled at him a couple of times, reassuring him that she was all right. Laine wondered if he had purposely kept a bit of distance between them during the proceedings. Since their encounter at her apartment he seemed to be trying not to crowd her in any way. If he was out to prove a point about not making any demands on her, his tactics were working. The only problem was that she missed him. As much as she had hoped that their moment of intimacy would not change their relationship, she could see that changes were already happening—for both of them.

Clay was not the only one behaving differently. Laine found herself seeing Clay with new eyes. She had always viewed him as a very attractive man, but his virile appeal had become strikingly obvious and she was terribly disconcerted. Their relationship had felt so safe before, as though Jim's unclarified status kept him alive enough in Laine's mind to protect her from consciously responding to Clay's sensuality. But the last few nights, as she lay in bed, she hated herself for so vividly remembering the feel of Clay's embrace, his warm, passionate kiss. The guilt stabbed right through her.

After the ceremony, a large group of people went back to MIA headquarters for a quiet gathering. Ted Lawrence, who had stood beside Laine at the funeral, kept close by at the reception. His presence helped Laine, his quiet strength and gentle support a great comfort. Finally, as family and friends began to leave, Ted came up to her and took her hand.

"You know, Laine, my saddest regret beyond losing my son is not having you for a daughter-in-law. You are a wonderful, caring woman and you would have made Jim a marvelous wife."

For yet another time that day Laine could feel her eyes begin to water. She squeezed Ted's hand, unable to say a word.

"Can someone who loves you give you some well-meaning advice?" he asked softly.

Laine nodded, a small smile breaking through her tears.

"Mourn Jim's passing and then be done with it, Laine. You have your whole life in front of you. It's time to let Jim rest in peace. Put his memory away in a corner of your heart and begin again. You have so much to offer. I know Jim would have wanted you to be happy."

Laine, crying quietly, reached her arms up toward the tall, stately gentleman and encircled his neck in a light embrace.

"Jim was very lucky to have had such a wonderful father. There will always be a place in my heart for you as well as for Jim."

"Thank you, child," he said, touching her cheek affectionately. He bent down to kiss her and then bid her a final good-bye.

The office had cleared out during her talk with Ted. Laine looked around the empty room, wiping away her tears, then walked over to her desk and sat down.

She thought about Ted's heartfelt advice. It made so much sense. Why did it seem so hard to follow? All of a sudden a cold shiver of rage shot through her, and her angry thoughts spilled out. Why Jim? Why did you have to go and die on me? Everything was going to be so perfect, so easy. We had it all. We were so much in love. Damn you, Jim Lawrence, damn you for making me go through this horrendous pain and anguish!

She dropped her head into her hands, letting the sobs finally erupt. She cried for the sadness, the anger, the utter waste. And she cried out of fear—fear of being alone, fear of loving again, fear of a pain that she could not endure twice. The tears fell for a long while, but afterward Laine felt enormously better. She had allowed herself the full spectrum of her feelings, good and bad, and her tears had a cleansing, renewing effect. Reaching for a box of tissues, she groaned when she saw it was empty. As she opened her desk drawer, a man's handkerchief floated down on the tabletop.

"Try this."

Laine swung around to see Clay standing behind her.

"I—I thought I was alone." She flushed with embarrassment at her breakdown, wondering with a sense of panic whether her outburst to Jim had been spoken out loud or, hopefully, only thought. She had been so upset, she wasn't even sure.

Clay gave no hint of what he had witnessed. Smiling gently, he perched himself on the edge of the desk.

"Feeling okay now?"

Laine picked up his handkerchief and wiped her tear-streaked face. "Yes, I really do." She smiled, feeling suddenly shy.

"You look like hell," he said, but his searching eyes said something else.

"Thanks, pal," Laine grinned as her hands involuntarily swept up to her hair, the neat chignon of this morning now half undone. She had no idea how captivatingly beautiful she looked, tears and all. Clay felt an overwhelming desire to wrap her up in his arms, to embrace her satiny smooth skin, to recapture the feel of her glorious hair, to kiss away her salty tears and make those magnificent eyes sparkle with excitement. But he bit his bottom lip, fighting that need as he had while he'd watched her cry her heart out. As badly as he wanted her, this relationship was too important for him to make the same mistake twice. He had no doubt that she would respond to him if he did act on his own desires. But this victory would be as bitter as his last. No, she was still too vulnerable, still wrapped up in her sadness. And afterward she'd suffer the same sense of guilt. Yes, he wanted her desperately, but for them to have any chance at all, she was going to have to meet him halfway. She was going to have to admit to her true feelings for him. Remaining cool despite his inner turmoil, he casually ruffled her hair.

"I tell you what," he said, clearing his throat. His thoughts had produced a husky quality to his voice. "You pull yourself together a little bit, and I'll buy you a drink and then take you home. What do you say?" Even if he had decided not to take a head-on approach, he wasn't above using a little subtle manipulation to help matters along. He cast her his most engaging smile.

Laine responded as he had hoped. She grinned and said, "I'd say that sounds great. But only if I can find my brush and some extra pins to fix my hair." As she reached for her purse, Clay caught hold of her hand.

"Take the pins out. I like seeing that mane of yours blowing freely in the wind."

Her eyes held his for a moment, and then she slowly slipped each of the pins from her chignon, letting her hair cascade in shimmering waves around her shoulders.

With a touch so light Laine could barely feel it, Clay ran his fingers over the silky strands of her hair. His voice was low and caressing. "Now you look like yourself again."

Laine stood up abruptly and started toward the door. "Let's go." Her own voice was disturbingly husky as she spoke.

Laine sipped on a brandy in the quiet lounge while Clay worked on a Scotch on the rocks. Pensively, she concentrated on feeling the pleasant warmth of the liquid as it rolled down her throat. The late afternoon sun had finally broken through the clouds, its rays penetrating the smoky gray windows to cast odd little shadows on the bar.

Yawning, Laine quickly brought her hand up to her mouth. "I'm exhausted. It's not even three o'clock in the afternoon and it could be midnight by the way I feel."

"You should be wiped out," Clay observed. "Unless those dark smudges under your eyes are the new thing in makeup, my guess is that you didn't get too much sleep last night."

Laine sighed. She had faced the fact this morning that there was going to be no amount of makeup that would camouflage her exhaustion. "It's funny," she said with no trace of a smile. "Last night I was so anxious and frightened about getting through the whole ordeal of a military burial. But being there today—I don't know—the experience felt alien, unrelated to Jim. He was such a casual, easygoing man. I think he would have much preferred a simple service in North Carolina where his body would be put to rest in a lovely countryside cemetery surrounded by familiar trees and hills. Today, standing at his grave in Arlington, I felt more removed from Jim than ever before."

"Maybe you're finally beginning to accept the fact that he's gone."

Laine frowned. "Clay, we haven't really had a chance to talk since that night in my apartment."

They both knew what night she meant.

Laine found it difficult to look directly at Clay. Lately his deep teal-blue eyes were so intense, so watchful. Forcing herself to face him, she again experienced that disconcerting sensation that he was seeing right through her.

"I've had the feeling you did not want to talk about our infamous moment of passion," he quipped sarcastically. He had thought he had successfully rationalized her rejection, but he realized he still hurt enough to strike back.

"You are developing a terrific talent, Clay Marsh, for making my blood boil," she snapped. "Maybe that kiss meant little to you, but—"

"But what? Don't tell me it meant something important to you? Other than causing you a strong jolt of guilt, that is." His tone was less harsh, even though there was still a bite to his words.

Laine felt the sting, but she also understood the pain behind his anger. "What is important to me," she said quietly, "is that we stop feeling all of this tension. I hate it."

Clay reached across the table and caught hold

of her hand. "Listen to me, Laine. I've been carrying a torch for you for a long time. I just can't douse it anymore. And right now it's blazing. So if you want me to tell you what I think about that other night, let me tell you this. I want a hell of a lot more from you than one furtive kiss and a momentary embrace. A hell of a lot more."

Laine opened her mouth to speak, but Clay cut her off. "Save the lecture. I'm not going to force you into anything. I'm also not going to pretend I don't want you. Right now all I'm asking you to do is sort out your feelings. But"—he pressed her hand more tightly—"be honest with yourself, Laine. Even if you can't be honest with me right now, be straight with yourself."

He downed the rest of his drink in one swallow. "Let's go," he said coolly.

"I thought you said you were taking me to lunch." Laine had to shout to be heard in Clay's silver Spitfire convertible. She really didn't mind the drive. In fact, Clay had granted her a strongly needed reprieve from work. She was pleased he had finally called, having decided that if he didn't contact her by today, she would call him. Almost a whole week had gone by since their uncomfortable encounter after the funeral. They were beginning to collect such encounters. Today would probably be no better. Again she wished for the return of their easy camaraderie.

Resting her head against the back of the supple tan leather seat, she closed her eyes, letting the warm rays of the sun bathe her face and the gentle wind tousle her hair. Was she going to spend her life wishing for the past to reappear? She was beginning to see how much safer she felt protected by her memories. The past was secure. The present and the future were much scarier.

They had been driving for a half hour along a lovely country road on the outskirts of town. She pushed a strand of hair away from her eyes. Clay glanced over at her for a moment and grinned. Then he focused his eyes back on the road, humming a familiar show tune.

Turning her head slightly to study Clay through squinting eyes, she realized that he had planned the drive to give her this time to unwind. Once again she was struck by Clay's sensitivity and depth of understanding. She studied him appraisingly as he drove. He had tossed his tie and jacket into the trunk and his casual appearance gave him a more naturally rugged look. His sharply etched profile was strong and confident. In the tight confines of the car Laine was acutely aware of his broad, muscular back and his lean, hard thighs. They grazed shoulders slightly as he occasionally shifted gears, and Laine found herself very conscious of his subtle touch, the texture of his skin, the appealing scent of his aftershave. She was finding it very difficult to ignore Clay's masculinity. Chastising herself had little impact. Those tingling sensations persisted. She tried to concentrate on the passing scenery.

As Clay guided the car up a short paved driveway, Laine spotted a lovely carved wooden signpost indicating they had arrived at Silver Glen Inn. A few other cars were parked along the side of the charming white house that looked like a miniature version of Tara, the mansion from *Gone With the Wind.* It was so characteristically southern and regal even on this small scale that Laine smiled with delight.

"What a find!" she said as she swung her legs out of the car and took Clay's hand.

"Wait until you taste the food. The Glen's fried chicken should be the only fowl allowed the adjective *southern.* For those more refined, who don't like getting their hands greasy, they make the lightest-tasting salmon croquettes in the world."

"It sounds like you come here often."

"When the city starts closing in on me and I want to feel the magic of the South, I head over here at full speed." He laughed, taking her arm as they stepped up to the veranda.

The inside of the inn was as charming and gracious as the outside. Done in creamy linen white and emerald green, the spacious entryway imparted a feeling of warmth and pleasant coolness at the same time. Laine would have loved to walk up the elegant, curved staircase, but the hostess cheerfully led them off to the left into a small dining room. Laine noticed that there were several such rooms on the main floor rather than one large dining area. She liked the sense of intimacy and privacy the arrangement provided. There was only one other occupied table in the room. An older couple, their table cluttered with a camera, tour books, and maps, were finishing up their lunch. The decor here was country south, with warm hickory wood walls and pine floors. Fragrant bouquets of summer daffodils, wild pink roses, and delicate white baby's breath decorated each white-clothed table.

Clay and Laine sat by a bay window that looked out on a rolling field sprinkled with wild flowers. Laine was acutely aware of the romantic setting this place created. She was also aware of the tension she was still working hard at ignoring.

They both ordered the southern fried chicken. "This really better be finger-licking good," she warned.

"If not, I promise to personally lick every one of those pretty fingers of yours clean as a whistle." He'd said it as a joke, but the sensual imagery struck them both at the same time.

Laine was relieved when the waiter brought their salads. As they started talking about a variety of subjects that were light and safe, Laine began to relax. By the time they dug into the chicken they seemed to have regained their old equilibrium. Over coffee and dessert Laine's conversation took a more serious path.

"I've been doing a lot of thinking these past few days," Laine said.

Clay was hoping her thoughts had been about the two of them, and he hid his disappointment when she added, "About what I'm going to do in the future. I keep wondering about whether or not to stay with the organization now. The thought of leaving makes me feel guilty." Her eyes quickly shot up to see if Clay's glance would be mocking, but his eyes reflected only interest. "I would be running out on all the families and loved ones of those men still missing. The problem is I feel so drained. I don't know if I have it in me to give more talks, fight more red tape, and," she added, a look of pain crossing her features, "I really don't know if I can cope with any more grief. It's terrible to say after all of my friends rallied round me, but the idea of going through the same experience with them time and time again—it . . ." She was struggling so hard to fight back tears, that she couldn't finish.

It wasn't necessary. The look in Clay's eyes told her he understood what she was trying to say. He extended his hand across the table and clasped her clenched fist, gently prying her fingers open.

"You're finally starting to make sense. I'd love to see you get away from the whole thing. Why not go back to writing? I still remember those delightful children's stories you had published. You gave up quite a promising career."

"I haven't had any inspiration to write charming little tales for a long time." There was an edge of bitterness in her voice.

"I'd like to see your desire return," he said

pointedly. "I'd like to see you get back in touch with your real self."

"My real self," she snapped, her tone edged with hysteria, "as you put it, has spent almost five years working night and day for the MIA program. My real self is still struggling with the loss of the man that should have been my husband. My real self stopped believing in fairy tales the day the government sent me that telegram. So don't talk to me about my real self or my desires."

Clay leaned toward her, his dark eyes glinting. "Then you tell me it wasn't your real self that kissed me the other night. Tell me that there was nothing real about how your body responded to me, nothing real about your desire when I held you to me."

His voice was barely a whisper, but Laine felt every word pierce through her. It was no use protesting. That was as much a part of her real self as the rest. Even at this moment, as angry and scared as she felt, her body was betraying her with a yearning for Clay. She could feel her face become flushed, and she couldn't find any words in her own defense.

"Come walk outside with me for a while. I think we both need to cool off." He threw her a wry smile. Under his sensitive gaze Laine's face played out the emotions she was trying to hide. He easily read her secret longing. But the ability to arouse her, to conquer her, was not what Clay desired. He wanted her fully, with no fears, no doubts, and no other ties. Clay was a determined man who usually got what he wanted. Looking at Laine, he was afraid that this time he might fail. Her ties to Jim had grown even more intense over the years the soldier had been missing. In her despair Laine had woven a steel web around her heart. By keeping Jim's memory alive, she also kept all the suffering and pain of the last five years equally alive. And those memories were her best defense against allowing herself to take new risks.

Laine had agreed to the walk, hoping it would perhaps offer her some relief. They leisurely strolled along a path that wound around the field they had seen from the dining-room window. A gentle summer breeze softened the heat of the afternoon sun. For a while neither of them spoke.

Finally Clay looked over at Laine, whose face wore a slight frown. "What are you thinking about?"

Laine glanced quickly at him and then looked straight ahead again. In a wistful voice she said, "I wish we could be friends again."

"We've never stopped being friends," Clay said, admonishing her lightly as he took hold of her arm and turned her toward him.

"Oh, Clay, don't pretend my emotions aren't obvious. You know damn well I'm not feeling particularly sisterly to you anymore." The words came out in a frustrated cry.

"What are you feeling then?" he demanded, his hand unconsciously gripping her tighter.

But she didn't answer his question. Instead,

she confessed, "You're one of the biggest reasons I want to get away from the organization. I'm scared that I can't work with you anymore, not without—without something more happening between us."

"Something more *is* happening between us," he answered, holding her arm so she couldn't turn away. He leaned forward and kissed her lightly on the lips. "You know that as well as I do," he murmured into her ear.

Laine tilted her head back to look up at him, her eyes not wavering from his. She reached up and touched his cheek. Then suddenly her arms were around his neck and she was pulling him against her. Her gasp of desire was drowned out by their insistent kiss. Clay crushed her against his chest, his strong hands fiercely pressed into her back so that she could not escape. But Laine had no wish to escape. Her body clung to him, weak with a passion that seemed to consume her. It was Clay who was the first to break away.

"See what I mean." He smiled seductively. "That was merely a sample, my passionate beauty, of what is happening. Tell me you don't agree?"

His smile was infuriating. Again he had deliberately forced Laine to acknowledge her desire.

"What does this prove, Clay? That my body wants you. Okay, it does. You are a very sexy man. I must be one of a long list of women who would respond to your advances."

"Hold on a minute. I seem to remember you

doing a bit of advancing yourself." He cupped his hand under her chin and grinned.

Laine squirmed out of his grasp. "Okay, I did. Is that what you want? Maybe we ought to just get it over with then. Go to bed and be done with it." She glared at him defiantly, expecting Clay to be enraged at her angry proposition.

Instead, he smiled down at her as if she were a child having a temper tantrum. "Oh, believe me, Laine Sinclair, I intend to take you to bed, but not under those conditions. When you and I have sex, we are going to be making love, not consummating a dare. And you, my fiery lass, will participate body and soul." He lightly pressed his lips to hers, cutting off her attempted protest. Then, taking a firm hold of her hand, he led her back up the path.

An hour later, when Clay pulled up in front of Laine's apartment, they had both calmed down. Clay reached over and lightly caressed Laine's shoulder. "Laine, let's get away together for a while—give ourselves a fair chance to find out what's going on between us. We could go down to my sister's beach house. Remember how much you loved it when we visited Jess and her family there last summer?"

The idea of some time off to loll around on the beach in peace and quiet was very appealing. That weekend last summer had been delightful. But Laine was not clear whether Clay's sister was going to be there now. If she and Clay were alone together, the idea of the forced intimacy was distressing. She had already seen too many times how easily her body could betray her, and despite her cavalier suggestion that they go to bed, she no more wanted a casual fling with Clay than he did with her. It was a commitment that he wanted. And right now nothing terrified Laine more.

"Afraid you won't be able to handle it?" He needled her gently.

Of course that was exactly what she was afraid of, but she always did have difficulty resisting a challenge.

"I'll think about your invitation," she conceded with a grin. Then she grew serious. "I still have the ceremony at the Vietnam War Memorial next week. Once that's over, I'll let you know about the beach."

"Fair enough," he said lightly, knowing that the dedication was still another traumatic experience that Laine would need to get through. Hopefully it would be the last.

The low, half-buried black granite monument, so much smaller than the Washington and Lincoln edifices that flanked it on either side, made its own powerful statement. Shaped in a V, the stone held the names of over fifty thousand men etched on its face. All of these men had lost their lives in the Vietnam War.

Several newly carved names, James Lawrence among them, bore fresh witness to the tragedy of the war. Many dignitaries and families and friends of the deceased solemnly stood listening to the heart-rending speeches. Laine had decided not to be one of the speakers, letting Janet Ross, her assistant, represent the organization at the service. Over the past few weeks Laine had successfully begun to put the pieces of her life back in order. She was sleeping better, eating better, and generally feeling better. More than anything, she did not want to destroy the still delicate balance of her recovery and she was afraid that speaking today might have shattering effects.

Clay was at her side, holding her hand. She hadn't seen him all week and was glad to have him near today. Frequently, as they stood together listening to the moving and empassioned speeches, their eyes misted over, but the physical and emotional contact between them helped them through the arduous ceremony.

Later that evening Clay made Laine dinner at his apartment. Afterward they sat together on his couch drinking espresso and listening to a soothing Chopin etude.

Clay stretched his arm across the back of the sofa, his fingers casually toying with a silky strand of her hair. Laine looked over at Clay with a sweet smile. As Clay drew her to him with a gentle pressure on her shoulder, she moved closer, resting her head against his chest. He continued to stroke her hair in a warm, comforting way.

Laine sighed deeply. "At least all the rigamorole is over," she said softly against his shirt.

Clay patted her head gently. "You're a strong lady," he said admiringly.

"No, I'm not," she answered without moving. "I like to pretend I am, but inside I feel weak and scared. I'm talented at putting on a good front."

"Well, you don't have to put on any fronts with me—ever. And I still say you're strong."

Clay took her face in his hands, kissed her tenderly on her lips, and moved away. Laine eyed him with a gentle smile, then put her arms around the broad expanse of his shoulders and returned his kiss with one equally warm.

"We're quite a pair," he teased, lightly massaging her back, his face nuzzling her glorious hair.

She rested her head on his shoulder, her fingers idly toying with the collar of his shirt. "Why do you waste your time with me?" she asked softly.

"Why?" He studied her lovely eyes, her finely shaped nose, those full, sensual lips. He ran his fingers across the satiny smoothness of her bare arms. "Because you drive me totally wild; because I can't get you out of my mind no matter how hard I try; because, my sweet, I love you despite your fears and uncertainty and your maddening stubbornness."

"You're pretty stubborn yourself," she retaliated with a grin, but then she cut it off abruptly. "I want to be fair to you, Clay. I would be wrong to mislead you. I'm still all torn up about Jim. Oh, I know in time the pain will ease and I'll come to grips with it. Beyond that . . . I know I've begun to make a habit of giving you mixed messages. It's because I'm scared and confused. I'm all tied up in knots, trying to sort everything out."

"Laine, come down to the beach with me. Let's give ourselves a chance to be together away from all the turmoil and stress of this past month. Who knows, maybe the sea air will help undo some of those knots?"

"And I suppose you intend to try doing a little of the untying yourself." She laughed.

"It was my best skill as a boy scout." He grinned back. "Will you come then?"

After a moment's hesitation she nodded her head in assent. Clay was well aware of her ambivalence about her decision, but he chose to ignore it. Instead, he stroked her hair, planting a tiny kiss on the top of her head. "You won't be sorry."

Clay sounded so confident that Laine almost believed him.

CHAPTER FOUR

Every time Laine closed her suitcase, another item she'd forgotten flew into her mind. She hurried to the linen closet to grab a tube of shampoo. Her attack of forgetfulness made little sense, considering all of the traveling she had done in her job for the past five years. She usually could organize and pack her things for a trip with her eyes closed.

But, she reminded herself, releasing the catches on the soft cowhide suitcase and fitting the shampoo into the toiletry pouch, this was no business trip. She wasn't even sure it was going to be a pleasure. Ever since agreeing to go with Clay to Virginia, she had fought back her reservations. She told herself it was important to resolve their relationship, not to leave ends dangling. Laine had half convinced herself that what she wanted was to work at recapturing their old friendship. She imagined that she could keep her attraction to Clay under control, make him understand that she did not want another serious involvement.

As long as she was daydreaming, her resolves came easily. She could play down the fierceness of her physical attraction for Clay, the astounding response her body had to his touch. When he wasn't around she had no trouble separating her body's desires from her determination to keep their relationship platonic. Her goal was to stay uninvolved, not go through any more hurt or grief. Alone she could convince herself that this was what she wanted. But would she still be convinced after spending a week with Clay?

As she shut her suitcase again, she let out an unladylike curse. She'd forgotten to pack her rain slicker. Throwing open the lid, she marched out to the hall closet to get the coat, vowing that if she'd forgotten anything else she would have to survive without it. She really did have to get her act together.

The doorbell rang just as Laine slipped her raincoat off the hanger. Tossing it over her arm, she went to open the front door.

"Expecting a storm?" Clay's dark blue eyes gazed at her playfully. It had to be close to ninety outside under a clear azure sky. Clay, looking very sporty in a blue-and-white striped T-shirt and slim-cut white chinos, stepped inside.

"Very funny," Laine muttered, walking back toward her bedroom. "This is positively the last thing I'm packing." She left the door open as she folded the slicker into the suitcase and closed it with determination. She wiped some beads of sweat from her brow. Despite the air conditioning, she felt uncomfortably warm.

Clay stood in the doorway watching her. He looked so relaxed and cool. Laine, keenly aware of her moist palms and the knot that was growing steadily tighter in her stomach, sat down on the bed.

"Oh, Clay, what am I doing? It's crazy for me to go away with you. Look at me. I'm a wreck."

"You look good to me." Clay grinned boyishly and walked into the room.

"Come on, be honest. Isn't that what you've been telling me? You know as well as I do that if I spend this week with you, we're just going to get in deeper."

He laughed at the unintentional double meaning in her words, but when she didn't laugh back, he came and sat down beside her.

"Laine, I have been honest with you. I told you I'm in love with you and I can't imagine a better way to spend this week than watching you discover you're in love with me. But I'm not planning some grand seduction. We know what I want. It's time you figure out what you really want." He stood up, catching hold of her slender wrists and pulling her up after him. "And until we both know that, your virtue is secure," he said, raising his hand in mock promise.

"You seem pretty confident that I'm going to figure out what I want," she said, furrowing her brow.

"I plan to help in every way I know how," Clay quipped.

"That's what I'm afraid of," she retorted, tugging her wrists free from his grasp.

"Relax." Clay reached for the suitcase and swung it off the bed. "If it makes you feel any better, my sister and her kids are staying down at the house as well. You couldn't ask for better chaperones." He had walked to the door with the suitcase. Turning back to her, he said, "So you see, I am not whisking you to the shore simply to have my way with you," he announced with a wry smile.

Laine cast him a bemused look. "I must admit you do baffle me at times."

Clay had laughed. "Well, I'd better confess. The cottage was supposed to be mine for the week. But Jessie called me last night saying her plan to go to Europe with David was off. She asked if I would mind if she and the kids came down to the beach for a few days."

"Thanks for restoring my faith in woman's intuition." Laine grinned. The tension had vanished and, shutting the door to the apartment, she began to really look forward to the trip.

The drive down to Virginia took a little over an hour. A few minutes before they reached the house Clay told Laine more about Jessie's sudden decision not to go away with her husband.

"Jess told me she's thinking about a separation. She and David haven't really gotten along for quite a while. It's not that they fight or even get into arguments. Actually David is always off somewhere, so they're never together long enough to fight. They would probably be better off if they did. Jess says the emptiness of it all is finally getting to her. So she may be kind of uptight this week, although, if I know my sister, she'll probably be a master at covering up her emotions."

Laine had met Clay's sister and brother-in-law along with their kids last summer when she and Clay had spent a weekend with them here at the beach house. Clay's news was not really surprising. Even in that short time last summer Laine felt a tension between the couple. David Collier was a career diplomat, and from all Laine could see, his work was everything to him. That weekend was supposed to be a vacation, but he spent almost the entire time either on the phone to Washington or overseas, or else he locked himself up in the den for hours at a stretch. Laine hardly saw him, and his own family did little better. She remembered thinking at the time that she could never tolerate such an empty marriage. His wife had finally come to that same conclusion. Laine felt sad for the whole family. In the end they would all suffer.

They turned into a newly paved private lane. The house itself sat less than a hundred yards from an exquisite sandy beach. There were no other homes in sight. It was one of the most secluded, idyllic spots Laine had ever seen. She adored the large two-story whitewashed cottage. Though it was built only a few years ago, Jess, who had designed it and supervised its construction, had been adamant about keeping the place casual and homey and not allowing any flashy modern touches. Laine thought the cottage was perfect. The house might have stood there perched on the sandy soil for a hundred years. She loved the ageless quality and had told Jessie so when they first met last year. Jessie beamed, telling Laine she couldn't have given her a better compliment.

Laine thought that she and Jessie might have become good friends had both their lives not been so hectic. She looked forward to seeing Jessie and the children again. Bonnie and Seth were lively, exuberant kids who had that special southern charm about them that Laine found both familiar and delightful. She wished she could be getting together with them under better circumstances.

Bonnie was the first one to meet the car as they pulled up at the house. Clay barely had eased his large frame out of the sports car before she was leaping at him. He gave her a big bear hug and a loud, smacking kiss on the cheek. All of a sudden Bonnie flushed as her eyes caught Laine's. Bonnie was close to twelve, that awkward age where one minute you were working hard at being very grown up and the next you were an uninhibited child. Now the attractive blond girl smoothed down her shirt and grinned self-consciously. It was a funny grin, but then Laine caught a quick flash of silver metal against Bonnie's teeth and understood completely.

"Hi, Laine. Mom's expecting you guys. She's

holed up in the kitchen trying to make an apple pie for dessert tonight." She threw Clay a wry smile, Clay grinning back knowingly. To Laine, Bonnie explained, "Every now and then Mom decides to go domestic. This is one of those times. I'm giving you fair warning—if I were you, I would definitely skip dessert."

"Come on." Laine laughed. "What could she do to an apple pie?"

"Well, let's see." Bonnie grinned impishly. "Last time she tried one, she forgot to peel the apples."

"I heard that!" Jessie, a tall, elegant woman as fair as Clay was dark, but with those same vibrant teal-blue eyes, came up behind them. In an overly large striped apron draped over a sophisticated lilac silk dress, she looked enchantingly comical.

"These apples have been stripped naked, I promise," she announced emphatically. With a warm chuckle she gave Bonnie a light pat on her bottom, hugged Clay and Laine, and ushered them both into the house.

"Since you've already started getting warnings, I might as well caution you about the rest of the meal. Seth has been down at the beach all morning, determined to catch our supper tonight. Something tells me you-all may be forced to eat my pie," she said, deliberately accentuating the southern drawl. "It might be all there is to eat. Actually, if he does catch something, things could get worse. David was always the one to clean the fish. I'm prepared to deal with fish only after they look like chicken cutlets."

Laine noticed the slight falter in Jessie's speech when she mentioned David's name, but Clay's sister had been quick to brush it aside.

"Don't worry," Clay said lightly. "I'll take on everything Seth manages to pull out of the ocean." He gave his sister an affectionate squeeze, and Jessie returned it warmly.

Supper that night went much better than any of them expected. Seth miraculously caught a large red snapper, aided by Clay, who had run down to the shore to give his nephew a hand. Seth beamed with pride as everyone heartily ate every last drop of the perfectly filleted fish. Even Jessie's pie, though it turned out a bit lop-sided, tasted delicious. Seth and Clay competed for who knew the most fish jokes, but it was Jessie's true stories about her and Clay's child-hood adventures and misadventures that kept everyone laughing hilariously. Bonnie, clearly taken with Laine, maintained a poised expres-sion, trying to impress Laine with her sophistica-tion and maturity. Finally she dropped the pretense and joined in with gleeful participa-tion. It was a perfect evening.

"You're up early this morning."

Laine brushed the sand off the palm of her hand and, shielding her eyes, she squinted up at Clay. She laughed as he came into focus.

"That's quite a T-shirt," she exclaimed. It was

bright yellow with black lettering across the front that read SAY UNCLE.

"You'll never lose me in a crowd with this on. Bonnie and Seth presented it to me this morning. We have this running contest about who can find the zaniest gifts for one another. This beauty is definitely up for first prize. I promised them I'd wear it today."

"Well, the color is very becoming," she chuckled.

Clay dropped down on the blanket beside her. She did not miss his not-so-subtle scrutiny of her attire either—at least what there was of it. The scant black bikini certainly hid few of her assets. Clay leaned over, pressing his lips against her shoulder. Laine responded with an involuntary shiver.

"Mmm. You're very warm. How long have you been out here?" He ran his fingers lightly down her spine, grinning when Laine abruptly edged out of his reach.

She regarded him ruefully. "I've been up since dawn, lazybones. There is something miraculous in this sea air. I can feel myself starting to rejuvenate already. And I don't think there's a sight more beautiful in this world than the sun rising over the ocean."

"Oh, I think I could think of at least one," he said, smiling seductively.

"Go for a swim?" she asked, to change the subject.

"I thought you'd like to do some water skiing this morning. I promised to take you out last summer, but the speedboat was out of commission, remember."

"I remember." Laine smiled. "I also remember my feeling of relief. I haven't been on skis for almost six years."

"Well, it's too late for excuses. Jess told me the old boat is purring like new and I think it's time for you to start . . ." He hesitated for a moment, giving her a telling look. "I think it's about time you began doing some of the things you used to enjoy."

With an irritating grimace she asked, "How do you always manage to know what's best for me?"

"Now, now." He grinned, refusing to respond to her gibe. "No use trying to wheedle out of it. Anyway, it's no different from bike riding. Once learned, you never forget how." He gave her another one of his infuriatingly sensual smiles.

"Very amusing," she snapped, but her glittering eyes indicated her acquiescence. "Okay, I'll try out my sea legs again. But just remember, Mr. Marsh, if I break any bones, you'll be receiving the doctor bills."

A short while later, in starting position, Laine felt the old rush of excitement she used to experience when she water-skiied. Growing up in a southern coastal town, it and surfing were her natural sports. She kept them up all through college. They had been completely forgotten once Jim had gone overseas.

"Are you ready?" Clay shouted from the motorboat.

With a wide grin Laine shouted back, "Easy does it now."

He waved back with a thumbs-up sign.

True to his word, he took her for a controlled spin around the inlet, keeping an eye on her to make sure she was okay. Laine returned the thumbs-up sign. She was doing better than okay. Clay had been right once again. She was having a great time, the old skill coming back to her readily. Feeling very confident, she urged Clay to speed up.

Clay did as she bid, watching with admiration as Laine began doing some fancy turns and jumps. She looked so utterly graceful and beautiful, so full of enthusiasm, Clay could literally feel his heart begin to pound in his chest. He congratulated himself on getting her to come down here with him. Already he could see the transformation in Laine beginning to show.

As she continued to encourage him to go faster, he pushed the throttle fully open, making the boat take a sudden leap forward. When Clay turned around to catch her reaction, he saw, instead, two empty skis and a tangled line. He instantly cut the engine, bringing the boat about. Scanning the water anxiously, he sighed with relief as he saw Laine swimming toward him. Jumping off the boat, he reached her with long, easy strokes.

"What happened?" He laughed, once he saw she was fine. "Couldn't handle the speed?"

"It wasn't that." She grinned. "That last jolt you threw me ripped the tie of my bikini top.

One half of a very expensive little suit is floating about somewhere in this inlet." She warned as he started to smile, "And don't you dare say anything smart."

He laughed loudly, paying no attention to her frown. "Well, beautiful, what now? Do you intend to bob around all day or get on board and risk . . . a sunburn!"

"Oh, shut up," she snapped, swimming with a purposeful splash toward the boat. She could hear Clay laughing behind her as she pulled herself on board. As Clay started to lift himself up, she shoved him back into the water, her turn to laugh.

"Oh, no, Clay. You aren't getting in this boat until you find my missing top."

"What?" he said, eyeing her with a blatantly lecherous grin. Her full, firm breasts, startlingly white against the rest of her creamy skin, struck Clay as purely exquisite.

Expressing his thoughts out loud, he said "Now I'm convinced there is a sight more beautiful than the rising sun." He wasn't laughing anymore.

Laine's laugh faded too. The scene was rapidly changing from playful to erotic.

"There really is no way I'm going to find that top," he mused and waited for her to concede the point. She stepped back, letting him hoist himself up onto the boat.

As he did she realized he was still wearing his bright yellow shirt.

"Wait a minute," she said with a teasing grin.

"A true friend would surely give a needy soul the shirt off his back."

He glanced down at his dripping wet shirt. Shrugging, he pulled it off. Laine reached out for it, but as she caught hold of one end he held on to the other, tugging her against him.

The startling sensation of their cool, wet bodies pressed so tightly together made them both momentarily breathless. In a husky voice Clay whispered in her ear, "Say uncle first."

Laine couldn't say a word. She was totally absorbed in the feel of Clay's powerful body, well aware of the force of his desire. Her lips against his chest, she could taste the saltiness of the sea on his skin. She released the shirt and let her hands travel slowly up his strongly muscled arms to his shoulders and then around his neck. With her tongue she began to taste the salty tang more avidly.

Clay eased Laine away, just far enough for him to bend down and capture first one then the other perfect pink nipple. With increasing pressure his lips and tongue urged the tender peaks erect. Laine's skin flamed with a heat that had little to do with the sun overhead. She blazed with a desire that seemed to engulf her. Every nerve ending tingled, every spot Clay fondled with his hands, his lips, his tongue, generated new sparks.

Together they slid onto one of the bench seats at the side of the speedboat. The small craft rocked precariously. They both laughed as some water spilled into the boat and onto the seat.

"I don't think these boats were designed with this in mind. Let's get back to shore," he whispered, a mixture of humor and need in his tone.

He held her close to him as he raced back to the beach, anxious that her doubts and fears might resurface, afraid that her desire would give way to guilt. But Laine was consumed with yearning. The heat of his body alone as he cradled her against him kept her passions stirred.

"What about your sister—the kids?" she asked, thinking about slipping on his shirt.

"Gone for the day. They're probably off shopping for some more crazy gifts." He laughed, easing the boat to shore. As he lifted her in his arms and carried her out onto the warm sand, he looked down admiringly at her.

"Did anyone ever tell you that for a little bit of a thing you've got the longest, most dynamite legs there ever were?"

Laine froze as Clay released her. Her eyes flooded with devastating sadness. "Jim always said that to me," she whispered.

Clay, too, became rigid, the desire in his dark eyes flashing to ice. Laine was desperate to get away. She swung around and started to run toward the cottage.

"Oh, no," Clay's voice erupted in a low, threatening growl, his hand roughly grabbing her by the elbow, spinning her back around. "I'm not going to let you run back to your memories. A minute ago you could think of nothing else but completing what we had begun. It wasn't Jim you were thinking about when you were wrapped around me out there, was it?" He practically screamed the question, the passion back in his eyes, but this time it was twinged with a cold rage.

Laine tried to struggle out of his viselike grip. Her fighting only resulted in the two of them falling heavily onto the sand, Clay on top of her. The pressure of his body against hers reawakened her own desire despite her anger. "Please, Clay," she begged. "Not like this. Don't." Tears sprang from her eyes.

But Clay was beyond listening. He felt driven to exorcise Jim from Laine's mind. He couldn't hear her plea, especially when her body was saying something so different. Her responses were telling him all he needed to hear.

Clay's lips smothered her gasps of protest, his tongue invading her parted lips. Hard fingers, powerful and determined, again explored her firm breasts, her taut, hard nipples echoing the desire she fought helplessly to control. An insistent yearning coursed through her trembling body as her mind waged its battle. Clay's movements grew slower, more deliberate as he felt the change in her. Laine began to lose hold of the anger, her mind able to concentrate on nothing but Clay's probing touches. Her hands spread against his powerful chest no longer struggled to push him away. The strong, pulsating beat of his heart resonated on her palm. Her own heart was beating wildly too.

"Oh, Clay, I want you." The words sprung from a yearning she could no longer fight. "I want you to touch me, caress me, make love to me," she murmured, punctuating her words with frantic kisses on his chest, his throat, finally his lips.

Clay's embrace became less fierce, his rage giving way to a tenderness born of Laine's admission. He returned her kiss, his tongue erotically probing her mouth and then lightly skimming across her parted lips.

Alone on the deserted beach, the warm sand a sensual cushion for their passion, the salty ocean breeze a delightful shield from the sun, Clay and Laine reached out for each other with utter abandon.

Releasing the ties of her bikini bottom, he tossed it to his side. He covered her body in an endless variety of kisses, his probing fingers tracing the sensuous curves of her exquisite silken flesh. Laine responded to his caresses with soft breathy moans of pleasure, her hands beginning their own journey of exploration.

She reveled in the feel of his hard, strong body, letting her hands press down his back and then up to his shoulders and neck. Her fingers plunged into the thickness of his dark wet hair, and as she thrust her hips against him, he caught hold of her and turned her over onto her back. With an expert mastery that drove Laine to the edge of desire he found and took possession of every sensitive inch of her body. He drove her on to even greater heights of pleasure, to a point where she almost felt insane with desire. She was spinning inside a turbulent whirlpool, going faster and faster.

When he kissed her now, she cried out with a frenzied need for him to take her fully. Her hands trembled as they slid down his back, and reaching his hard, firm buttocks, she dug her fingers into his flesh, grinding him against her.

Clay's hand intimately slid between her slender legs, gently parting them. Then, easing his full weight on top of her, he entered her, his own feverish desire as great as Laine's. As the riveting intensity of their passion soared, they moved together with an instinctive, age-old rhythm, finally reaching the crest of the wave, the ecstatic sweetness of their release causing them both to cry out with joy.

For a few moments they lay motionless, all energy spent; yet the desire to remain one was still vibrantly alive. Laine's fingers lightly glided up Clay's back. She enjoyed the feel of the rippled muscles as her hands moved upward.

"I love the ways you touch me," Clay whispered in her ear. "I never thought I could ever love someone so strongly." His voice caught in his throat as he saw the red marks on her arms where he had grabbed her so roughly. Tenderly he kissed the reddened spots. "My God, I must have gone mad for that moment. I had to have you . . . I . . ."

"Shh," Laine whispered. "It's all right. You only forced what I wanted—what we both wanted—and had to finish."

Gently he eased off her. He cupped her chin,

guiding her head toward him as he lay on his side gazing at her. "I love you so much, Laine. There's even more power behind those feelings than I understood. Making love to you has not finished anything. It's only a beginning."

The sound of tires on the gravel driveway around the other side of the house signaled Clay's sister's return. Clay slipped on his trunks and reached into the boat to get the shirt for Laine. He smiled devilishly, recalling the beginning to this whole astonishing interlude. Laine grinned back, knowing exactly what he was thinking.

He waited for her to put her things on, but when he offered her his hand, she said softly, "Go on ahead. I'll be up in a little while."

A flash of displeasure creased his brow.

"Have a heart." She laughed lightly. "I don't think your niece and nephew are going to understand the sudden switch in ownership of this shirt."

He bent down and caught hold of a wayward strand of her glistening hair. Tucking it behind her ear, he said, "Promise me you're not going to sit down here having pangs of regret."

She looked up at him, the tender look of love in his eyes impossible to dismiss.

"I promise," she said, warming his cheek with a caressing touch. He held her hand there for a moment, then stood up and walked along the sand to the glistening white cottage.

CHAPTER FIVE

The gentle rolling waves lapped against the shore, small rivulets of water skimming along the sand, lightly spraying Laine's feet. She watched the procedure for several minutes, her mind wholly absorbed in the ebb and flow of the current.

She had promised Clay not to sit there allowing herself feelings of regret. It turned out not to be a difficult promise to keep. She honestly felt no remorse. Her conscience did not torment her with self-recriminations. There were no misgivings, in that sense.

She had wanted Clay with as much fervor as he had wanted her. At last she had been able to accept her feelings and, now, having allowed herself to express those desires, she felt in some way a relief. And the experience of making love with Clay had gone beyond all her fantasies.

It was this very realization that was causing the problem. As she sat looking out on the water she found herself unable to stop making comparisons between her relationship with Jim and those freshly etched moments of tumultuous passion shared between her and Clay. There was simply no way around it, no way to rationalize it. Never with Jim had Laine ever experienced the intensity of feelings that Clay had unleashed. No amount of telling herself that Clay was merely older and a far more experienced lover convinced her that was all there was to it. She knew that her own responses to Clay were not the result of Clay's skillful technique. No, there was something far deeper that had caused the fiery eruption of passion in both of them.

She was in way over her head. Her ability to sort out what was happening to her seemed overwhelming. She had promised herself over and over again to keep up her guard. Now, just as the pain of losing Jim was finally easing, she was stepping into deep water all over again.

No, she did not regret what she and Clay had shared together. But she also had no intention right now of letting it happen again. With a resolute step she walked back up to the cottage.

As she quietly let herself in the back door, she saw Clay leaving the house with his niece and nephew. She could hear Jess humming to herself in the kitchen, no doubt whipping up another dessert concoction now that she had proven her culinary skills. Laine smiled and went upstairs to shower and change.

After she slipped into a beige print sundress, she picked up Clay's T-shirt and dropped it off in his room on her way downstairs. She was not going to be saying uncle again.

Jessie was just hanging up the phone when Laine walked into the kitchen. As Jess turned around to see who had walked in, Laine saw immediately that she had been crying. Her face, despite her tan, looked ashen.

"Jess, what is it?" Laine hurried over to where Jess was standing. She could feel the older woman's muscles tremble as Laine stretched out a comforting hand. Jess sank into a kitchen chair, dropping her head into her hands.

"It's Dave. He just called me from Geneva." She stopped abruptly, clearly trying to compose herself. Brushing her palm against her damp cheeks, she continued. "He's in the hospital."

"Oh, Jess," Laine said, pulling up a chair beside her and taking her hand. "What happened?"

Jess looked across at Laine. "He's all right," she said. "I didn't mean to let you think it was critical. He did have what he insists was a very mild heart attack. He must be telling the truth because they are planning to release him tomorrow."

"Thank goodness," Laine exclaimed with relief.

Jess continued to look at Laine. "He asked me to come meet him in Geneva. He said he wanted us to spend some time together, to talk, maybe to sort things out."

Laine was confused by Jess's manner. She would have thought Jess would jump at the chance to try to work things out in their marriage.

"Don't you want to go?" Laine asked softly.

"You would think there would be a simple answer to such a straightforward question." Jess smiled and then sat pensively for a few moments. "A year ago, even a couple of months ago, I could have answered you easily. Last year I would have been racing to his side, elated that he was finally ready to focus some of his attention on us for once." Jess brushed some imaginary crumbs from the table.

Looking down at her hands, Jess went on, her voice noticeably harsher. "Two months ago I could have given you an easy answer as well. I would have told you he could rot in hell before I would chase after him. I would have said it was far too late."

"Now," she went on, a puzzled frown on her brow, "I just don't know. It's funny, but watching you and Clay together is really what has stirred up so much ambivalence for me."

"Me and Clay?" Laine was surprised.

"I remember a time, oh, fifteen years or so ago, when David and I looked at each other in the way you and Clay do. We were very much in love with each other."

Laine's eyes widened even more. She was about to refute what Jess said about her feelings toward Clay. But Jess was already back on her own relationship with her husband, and Laine realized there was no point in having Jess see that she was not in love with Clay. Besides, she thought with a disturbing rumble from within, maybe she wanted to deny something that already existed. Refusing to think about it, she forced her attention back to Jessie.

"While I've been down here this past week trying to come to grips with separating from Dave, I've never felt so lonely. Oh, Laine, life is too short to spend it feeling sad and alone." It was advice she was giving herself, but it struck a deep chord in Laine as well.

"I've been realizing that all the years I spent griping about the fact that David was too busy with his career and had no time for his family—well, I've been as much to blame as him. I let myself get in my own ruts, letting the kids, all the volunteer work, even the campaigning for Dave, take up so much of my time. I told myself I had to keep busy to ward off the pain of loneliness. But, the truth is, it kept me from fighting for what I wanted."

Jessie's words continued to hit home for Laine. Hadn't she spent all these years drowning herself in work to keep the awful feeling of emptiness at bay? Wasn't she still doing that?

"Maybe it isn't too late for you and David."

"I think I'm afraid to find out. I never wanted things to work out more than I do right at this moment, but I'm scared. David has never felt so vulnerable. He's never had a sick day in his life.

Now he's not feeling so invincible. The idea of having his family at his side seems appealing. But I'm not naive enough to believe that a few weeks down the road he won't be madly embroiled in work again."

"But, Jess, aren't you telling me that you have as much responsibility for what happened in your relationship as David. Maybe you have to go after what you want instead of sitting back and hoping that he will come around."

Jess grinned. "You're a sharp lady, Laine. And you don't hold back any punches. I guess it is time to stop storing all my grudges in my back pockets and go after my man!"

Laine laughed. "You and your brother are a lot alike." Her laugh died quickly as Jess cast her a look full of awareness.

"When we were growing up I used to think that Clay was the only fighter. When he wanted something, you could bet your last buck he was going to get it. Good thing too. I'd hate to be around to watch the results if he were to fail. He's not what one would call a gracious loser."

Now it was Laine's turn to return the knowing look.

"Well," Jess said with her typical verve, "I better get packed and make a plane reservation." She smiled broadly at Laine.

"I really hope things work out for you, Jess. You deserve it."

"I could say the same to you," Jess answered, her tone serious. She hesitated for a moment, then sat back down at the table next to Laine. She took her hand, squeezing it affectionately.

"I'm not going to say I understand what you're going through, Laine. I always hate when people say that to me. It sounds so patronizing. But just imagining what it must have been like for you—waiting with fear and anxiety and dwindling hope all these years for your young man to come home to you . . ." Tears filled her eyes. "Only to learn in the end that he was dead." She spoke softly, her features reflecting so much empathy that despite Laine's best efforts, her own eyes began to water and she tried to wipe away her tears.

"Don't hide your tears or feel embarrassed, Laine. Like I said before, I won't pretend to say I know the grief you must feel, but I am a good observer. I can see that you and my brother share something very special together. I spotted it a long time ago. And my guess is that the two of you have a real chance for happiness. It isn't a crime to fall in love a second time. You were only a girl when you fell in love before. Being a woman in love can be a very different thing." Jess gave Laine a light but abrupt pat on the shoulder. "Look at me, playing Dear Abby. I'm the last one to talk, given my current relationship with David."

Laine reached out for Jess's hand. "Dear Abby doesn't hold a candle to you, my friend. And I think you really can understand what I'm going through. Maybe I just need time—time to get everything in perspective. Whatever happens,

Jess, I want you to know I appreciate your caring and sympathy. It means a lot to me. Clay means a lot to me, too, but I don't know what will happen. I've spent too many years trying to second-guess the future, always trying to figure out ways to break the odds. It didn't do any good. Now I think I'll take one day at a time."

Jess stood up. "That makes sense. I think I'll follow that advice myself." She gave Laine an assertive nod.

Laine walked with Jess out of the kitchen. After a warm hug Jess ran up the stairs and Laine decided to sit out on the porch for a while.

The midday sun seemed to pucker the air with its intense heat, but Laine managed to find a shady spot on the far side of the porch. She pulled over a white wicker rocker with a matching footstool and made herself comfortable. She leaned her head back and took a deep breath. So many thoughts and feelings were careening through her head that it was impossible to relax. Images of Clay and Jim kept flashing by. And then there were the images of herself six years ago when she was young and in love mixed in with visions of herself today.

Who was she now? What did she want? This morning there had been no doubt in her mind about wanting Clay. She had yearned for him with a passion that was almost foreign to her. Thinking about it forced her to reflect again on her relationship with Jim.

When she and Jim first became serious there had seemed to be so much time. They both treated their life together with a cavalier disregard for the future. And then the Vietnam War began to weigh down on them, forcing them to see a future possibly filled with danger. Friends were being drafted, people they knew were returning home injured. Others were killed. Laine often tried to share her fears with Jim, but he was determined to push aside the awful possibilities. He was much better at denial than Laine. She realized now, looking back on that time, how unreal much of it was. Pretending that life held no perils, that she and Jim would somehow bypass all difficulties, and like a fairy tale live happily ever after.

Fairy tales are for the very young, she chided herself, determined to keep from crying again. There had been enough tears. She was beginning to learn something very important. The time for dreams and fantasies was over. She was no longer a naive, innocent young thing afraid to face a future that seemed totally out of her hands. She had to face the future, but first she had to face the present. No more sitting back, no more waiting for the fates to deal out the cards. She had to take a grip on life, find a direction, and go with it.

She saw the kids and then Clay popping up in the horizon. Impulsively, she sprang up, hurried inside, and went up to her room. She felt as though she were on the track of something important and that seeing Clay right now would only increase the difficulty she was having following that track to its end.

* * *

The house was oddly silent the next morning. Lulled by the peaceful quiet, Laine closed her eyes again and drifted back off to sleep. A light rap on her door wakened her.

"Hey, lazybones." Clay's deep, laughing voice came through her door. "I thought you were the one who loved to watch the rising sun. Keep this up and you'll barely catch it sinking back down again. Besides, I've got a fabulous breakfast ready and it's getting cold fast."

Laine stretched. "Give me a chance to open both eyes," she grumbled.

"Nope, one will do. Hurry up."

She heard Clay's footsteps on the stairs. Even his step sounded cheerful and exuberant. Laine's fitful sleep punctuated by graphic nightmares left her frame of mind anything but bubbly. However, she obeyed Clay's demand. Hurrying out of bed, she dressed quickly and went down to the kitchen. The marvelous aroma of frying bacon wafted toward her as she swung open the door. Clay, his back to her, was expertly flipping the golden brown slices, smoothing them back down on the cast-iron griddle.

"Where is everybody?" Laine thought she would get a chance to see Jess and the kids this morning before they left.

Clay turned to her, grinning. "We are everybody."

Laine was struck by how much younger Clay looked this morning. There was a carefree, gentle quality about him that she had never seen before. He slid the bacon onto a dish near the stove and then walked up to her. As he drew near, Laine could feel herself tighten and she stepped back. Clay noticed it immediately and stopped in his tracks. A flash of annoyance altered his features, but then it was gone.

Give her time, he cautioned himself. Don't make things happen too fast. She's bound to be a little tense and on edge. He backed off, returning to the stove.

"How do you like your eggs—scrambled or fried?" His tone was light and easy again, but Laine knew this time it was forced. With her new philosophy of taking one day at a time, she hadn't given any thought to what seeing Clay this morning would be like. She doubted she would have felt prepared anyway. His effusiveness and the positively glowing look of love in his eyes had thrown her more than she could have guessed. That look told her in no uncertain terms that yesterday had marked a turning point in their relationship, at least for Clay. As for her, yesterday had created only more confusion and an ambivalence that still needed to be sorted out.

"Scrambled," she said finally, more for something to say to break the potent silence than because she had an appetite for any breakfast.

Clay came over to her. "You don't sound like a hungry woman." His words clearly conveyed a double meaning. Laine felt slightly dizzy as his eyes gazed so knowingly into hers. His confrontative style shouldn't have surprised her. He always did come right to the point.

"Clay, please don't rush things." Her pleading look sparked another flash of anger that Clay barely managed to keep under control. With the anger came a sense of helplessness. It was not a feeling he liked. Throwing up his hands, he said, "All I had planned to do was feed you breakfast, not seduce you on the kitchen table. Even without my family here to chaperone you, rest assured I'll keep my pace as slow as you want."

"You don't have to be so damn facetious," Laine countered. "What do you want from me? My whole world is swimming around so fast I can barely keep my head above water. I envy you your ability to see everything in such easy terms. But our making love once doesn't mean my life is suddenly simple and clear. It's about as clear as . . . as mud."

She stormed across the room and ran out the back door. It slammed shut behind her. Clay didn't follow. They both needed time to cool off. He turned off the stove, took off the bacon, and dumped it into the trash. So much for a romantic breakfast.

When she got to the water's edge, Laine stopped running. Catching her breath, she slipped her feet out of her sandals and stood looking out to sea, trying to figure out just what she was running from. A light but steady wind whipped her chestnut hair against her cheeks. As she shook the wayward strands free of her face she began to walk slowly along the shore, letting the wet sand tug at her feet as the tide drifted out. The water felt colder today. The sun, swallowed up by somber, dusky clouds, offered none of that luxurious southern warmth this morning.

Laine was oblivious to the chill in the air, numb to the icy water spraying her feet. Running away. Yes, that was it. She was still running away. As she walked a straight path along the shore she realized that this was symbolic of what she had to do. She had to follow the path to its end. The end had not yet been resolved. Laine was still caught in a tangle of past and present, unable to separate one from the other.

A memory took hold. She and Jim walking together on an early spring day down at the beach near his folks' summer home. It was cold that day too. Jim had taken off his heavy tweed sweater, the one she had knit him that past Christmas, and insisted she wear it over hers. It had been much too big for her and they had both laughed as he pulled the bottom of the sweater down to her knees. Then he had taken the sleeves, hanging way below her hands, and tied them together behind her back.

"There, now you're my prisoner forever, to do with as I choose," he had exclaimed with a teasing leer. "And I have a perfect plan." He had scooped her up, fireman style, over his shoulder, and raced back with her to the cottage, Laine shrieking in playful outrage for him to untie her.

A strong gust of wind carried Laine back to

the present. Pushing her hair from her cheeks, her palms felt the hot tears on her face.

"Forever," her voice echoed loudly across the windswept sand. There was no forever and yet there seemed to be no end either. Again the outrage of it all consumed her with a pain that burned through her very soul.

Her tears transcended her own loss. She cried for all the vital young men who wanted so much from life, who offered so much to life, who ultimately offered themselves. Gone forever. In the end, that was the only forever. And the memories of who they were engraved forever on the hearts of those who loved them.

She had no idea how long she walked. A while back she noticed some light raindrops showering her gently, finding the sensation soothing. Hearing her name now being called against the wind, she turned around to see Clay running across the sand toward her. She stood motionless, waiting for him to reach her, wind-tossed strands of hair whipping against her face.

"Good thing you brought your raincoat after all." He held out the slicker she had remembered to pack that last minute. Looking at it curiously for a moment, she suddenly realized those gentle raindrops had increased to a rather forceful shower. The winds were gusting more adamantly as well, a full-fledged summer storm insistently brewing.

Clay had thrown on a sweater. Laine flinched as the memory of Jim grabbed her mind again.

Shaking her head of the vision, she took the raincoat and put it on.

"Have you worked up an appetite?" he asked with a gentle smile, adding, "No pun intended." He tucked a few strands of her hair behind her ear, but the wind freed them instantly.

Laine looked up at him, touched by the tenderness in his gaze. They started to walk slowly back toward the house. The storm was really getting a head up now, but neither of them hurried their pace.

"I've made an important decision, Clay." Laine had to raise her voice to be heard against the gusty wind. "I'm definitely leaving the organization. I see now that I have to go on from there."

"I've been hoping you would come to that decision. Will you go back to writing?" The relief in his voice was apparent. He firmly believed that the only hope for the two of them, and even for Laine herself, was to make that break—put the past in its proper perspective and go on to future plans and goals.

Laine stopped walking and took hold of Clay's hand. "Yes, I have decided to go back to writing."

He waited for her to go on. There was something in her tone that cautioned him to be on guard.

"Even though I honestly feel I need to leave the MIA organization, I'm just not ready to put it all behind me." As she saw Clay's scowl she looked steadily at him. Her voice was soft against the wind, but Clay, standing so close, heard every word. He stood silent, rigid.

"It isn't only Jim. I've spent all these years mourning so many men, so many lost lives. I have been through an experience that few people know about or understand. Don't you see, Clay? I have to somehow share what I've been through. I'm going to write about my relationship with Jim, what it was like to go through his being missing in action, what the MIA organization has done to try to help in the quest to find Jim and all those like him who suffered the same fate. It is something I have to do for me and for the others who've suffered like I have, or who will."

She searched Clay's face for understanding if not approval. But all she saw was cold rage, his features as stormy as the tempest growing wilder by the moment. They were both soaked, large streams of rain dripping down their faces. Clay's eyes darkened, holding her in his gaze. The ocean roaring behind them, the awesome, ferocious waves crashing turbulently against the shore, Laine felt a forbidding sense of danger. She turned away, but Clay grabbed her arm.

"I should get the prize for being the biggest damn fool of the century. I actually thought you were ready to start living again. You sure as hell felt alive on the beach yesterday."

Laine's eyes flashed with anger. "I am living, only not the way you want. I'm following my own path, one I think is best for me. I'm sorry if it doesn't meet your standards for living. But then yours do seem rather limited. Obviously a roll in the sand shows a lot more life than doing something meaningful and valuable with your time." Her rage was making her say things she didn't want to say—didn't even mean—but she couldn't stop. "I'm fed up with your selfish desires and your . . . your jealousy."

"And I'm tired of your neurotic need to cling to a dead man to protect yourself from one who's alive and kicking, and knows how to make you feel the same way."

"You bastard," she screamed, moving her hand in a swift motion, slamming it against his cheek. Clay caught her hand just as it landed.

Snatching her wrist, he sneered, "If you're so determined to keep Jim's memory alive, then remember something else." With that he seized her around her waist, forcing her other arm behind her back, and crushed her to him in a relentless, demanding embrace. His mouth bore down on hers with unyielding force and bruising passion, his tongue penetrating past her lips despite her struggles.

And then her struggles ceased. Held in his fierce grip, a flood of raw passion took possession of her, the violent storm around them nothing compared to the storm within. When he released her pinned hand, she immediately drew it around his neck, clinging to him with a burning hunger, her lips willingly obedient to his untamed craving.

Her body burst with the same blazing need it had yesterday. Only now the passion was fused with an almost violent longing to cast away everything but the moment they had captured. Whatever else might exist, Laine knew her fiery need for Clay was already deeply imbued within every fiber of her being. No man ever before or ever again would unleash this savage intensity of pure desire within her.

A flash of lightning streaked across the near-black sky at the very moment Clay roughly pushed Laine away from him. Stunned, Laine staggered back, fighting to regain her balance. She looked up into Clay's grim, smoldering stare, the raging storm adding potency to his dark, fearsome stance and the hard-edged gleam in his eyes.

"While you're busy fueling your memory of Jim, remember this too."

Shaken and drenched from the pelting rain, she felt the rage and agony of what had just happened envelop her as she stood motionless in the throes of the storm and watched Clay. It wasn't until he had faded out of view that she was able to regain some equilibrium and make her way back to the cottage.

CHAPTER SIX

By the time Laine got to the house, the storm had begun to mellow. Still chilled, shivering beneath her raincoat, she hesitated as she neared the front door. The possibility of another confrontation with Clay seemed more than she could bear right now. But there really wasn't any choice. If she didn't go indoors and get out of these wet clothes, she'd be courting a good case of pneumonia.

Squaring her shoulders, she opened the door and stepped inside. The house was silent. Not looking around, Laine headed straight upstairs to her bedroom. On her way, she noticed that Clay's door was open and that his bedroom was empty. There was no sign of him anywhere. She refused to give it any thought—except that she was glad he wasn't here to . . . To what?

Laine had always prided herself on her ability

to be self-contained. And over the past few years she had made it through more painful, trying times than she cared to count. For all the fears, the sleepless nights, the heart-rending pangs of loneliness, she had kept herself together, pulling in the reins of her emotions with a tight-fisted control. "Strong," Clay had called her. "A strong woman."

Her strength these last days seemed to be evaporating like puffs of smoke. She had nothing to grab on to, nothing to give her stability and focus.

No, that wasn't true. She reminded herself that she had decided on a focus. Her book. That would be her guiding line, her way to regain her strength and her balance.

Again the anger welled up in her. Why couldn't Clay understand? Lately he had become so pig-headed, so harsh and closed. She stripped off her wet things, tossing them across the room in a futile attempt to vent the frustration and anger consuming her.

Under the stinging hot shower her body relinquished some of its tension. As she soaped herself, her mind conjured up other images of Clay. His raw passion, his tender warmth, that special understanding and compassion. Those qualities had also emerged and grown stronger and sharper over these past few days. But Laine refused to dwell on these visions because they only complicated matters, as they'd been doing this whole while. Better to stay with the anger, she told herself. It was safer. It made her feel less vulnerable.

She bundled herself up in her terry robe and returned to her bedroom feeling at loose ends. Her small travel alarm told her it was only a little after eleven, but the sky outside was so dark and murky it might have been evening.

Not sleepy, she pulled some blankets out of the antique armoire and climbed back into bed anyway. There was warmth and comfort there. Curling up into herself, she pulled the thin wool covers up over her chin, trying to make her mind go blank. But thoughts of Clay held tight rein there, refusing to leave no matter how hard she willed them to vanish. She should never have come here with him. But something had nevertheless driven her to agree. Whom was she trying to fool? Since the first night after he'd told her about Jim, that blazing desire had erupted, and for weeks afterward she could find no way to extinguish the fire inside of her. Her need for him dispelled all fears, all rationalizations, all sense of what was best for her.

If she had not been prepared for the passion that would continue to ignite them, she was even less prepared for the anger and rage that had also exploded between them. Knowing and being witness to Clay's mercurial temperament in no way hinted at the fierceness he could demonstrate in his confrontations with her. And she with him. That was even more amazing. Laine Sinclair, cool, competent, feet on the ground.

Self-contained. Until now. Her own capacity for rage shocked her the most.

The covers, tossed over her head as they were, did not provide the safe, secure cocoon she had hoped to create. There was no hiding from her own thoughts and feelings. Bound up with so many memories of Jim, she was nevertheless being forced to come to grips with her overwhelming passion for Clay. Her feelings, both fiery and stormy, added dimensions to her personality that she had never before recognized. Clay was provoking emotions in her that went far deeper than merely physical responses to his sensuality. And as disturbing as they felt, there was undeniably a new excitement and energy being generated.

But her idea for this book about Jim and the MIA group was taking a firm hold in her mind. She was beginning to see it not only as a tribute and a chance to inform and enlighten the public. It was also something more basic—a chance for her to work through all she had experienced, to see it with a new and hopefully clearer eye. And then maybe, hopefully, lay the past to rest finally.

Throwing the covers off, she slipped on a pair of slacks and a light pullover sweater. Although she felt a lot warmer, there was still a nip in the air. Searching through the drawers of a small desk in the corner of her room, she found a pen and a few sheets of paper.

For several minutes she stared down at the empty white space, pen poised in hand. She tried to concentrate, encouraging her mind to cooperate and draw her back into the past. However, the present became more and more pervasive. Her eyes wandered out the window. The storm had stopped, but the skies hinted of another burst of rain readying itself at any moment. Her ears were tuned to pick up any sounds within the house. Any sounds of Clay. Where was he?

She walked over to the window and looked out. Her room faced the front of the house. Glimpses of the ocean could be spotted, but she couldn't get a clear view of the vast stretch of beach they had walked. Clay had to be out there somewhere since his car was still parked out front. Her anger at him was becoming tempered by concern. Clay was as soaked as she had been. He needed to get out of his wet clothes before he came down with something.

She didn't want to start sympathizing with him. She didn't want to feel compassion and understanding for his turmoil and anguish. Staying angry felt like her only protection. But it was useless. Thinking about him tore at her heart. Clay so wanted her to look ahead and couldn't tolerate her need to turn back and dwell in the past as she wrote her book. But she had to make some sense out of the past. And above all else, she owed this to Jim.

Clay's sneakers made squishing sounds as he walked. The storm had begun to die down, but he was familiar with these fierce summer rains and knew, despite the slackened wind, that another storm was just around the corner. He made no effort to turn back, to head home. He was oblivious to the chill dampness as his soaked sweater and jeans clung to his body.

In the distance, twinkling lights shone through the windows of scattered houses looking like faraway stars. The morning darkness had forced the night upon the day. The gloom fit Clay's mood perfectly.

Every now and then he paused, gazing out at the tempestuous waves tumbling, cascading, rolling over the sand in turns, their rhythm loud and emphatic. The rushing water slapped at his legs, tugging at him, forcing him to step back.

Clay loved the ocean in all its moods. Sometimes, bottled up in his city office, the pressures and frustrations of the day beating at him with a persistent hammer, he'd close his eyes and picture himself at the edge of the sea, letting the cool, ever-steady water and the salt air refresh and revitalize him.

Today the ocean offered no solace. He kicked at a gnarled piece of driftwood, walked by, and then abruptly turned back, stooping to retrieve it. He held it in his hand, tracing the twists and bends in the wood.

Really, he told himself, there were no answers. He wanted Laine. That much was simple and untouched by doubt. That, and loving her. He had known he loved her for a long time. His feelings had grown while he fought acknowledging them, the whole time he and Laine had tried so desperately to discover if Jim was still alive. He had never let himself think of Jim personally, separate him from all the other MIAs as Laine so understandably did. It was another part of his defense against rejection and pain. Until Jim's death had been confirmed he coped with his feelings by accepting the fact that Laine belonged to Jim. Never, consciously, had she ever led him to believe otherwise. Until now.

That was what was driving him crazy. That was what there were no answers to. The cloak of denial had been lifted for both of them. Their feelings had been spread out across this very beach that he now stood on. There was so much they could have together, so much they had already shared. They were just beginning. . . .

He tossed the driftwood into the ocean. It quickly disappeared, swallowed up by the raging sea. The rain was starting again. Large droplets splashed on his face. They felt like tears.

His footprints too had vanished in the sand, washed up by the turbulent waters. Clay turned his back to the sea and headed home.

The only light in the house shone from Laine's bedroom. Clay didn't turn on any others as he stepped inside. He'd grown used to the soft, overcast grayness. In the hall he tugged off his sodden sneakers, leaving them by the door. Walking into the living room, he stripped off his wet sweater and shirt, draping them over one of the sturdy Windsor chairs facing the fireplace. He threw some logs on the grate and struck a match to the neatly arranged kindling. The well-dried wood burned easily, a blaze quickly growing. Clay sat on the soft woven rag rug before the fire's warmth, his eyes mesmerized by the leaping flames. He ran his fingers through his wet hair, then, propping his elbows on his knees, he pressed his fingertips against his temples and closed his eyes. The light sound of footsteps on the stairs made him open them again, but he did not turn around.

Laine stood at the entry to the living room. Her eyes traveled over the back of Clay's head, across the broad expanse of his shoulders, down the ribbon of his spine. The fire cast a halo effect around him. Softly she walked across the room to where he sat. Just behind him, she hesitantly placed her hand on his shoulder. The heat of the fire made his skin feel hot. Still not moving or speaking, Clay pressed his own hand over hers. Slipping down onto her knees, she placed her other palm against the warmth of his neck. He took her hands, drawing them around to his chest and then he leaned lightly against her, the soft wool of her sweater comfortingly soothing. She smelled of lilac soap and apple shampoo. Just like a garden of delight, he thought, smiling.

Laine placed her cheek against his damp hair, pressing his weight more tightly to her breast. With her arms around him, they gazed together at the dancing, crackling flames. Neither of them made any effort to break the soothing silence. Even the storm had finally lost all its steam, the clouds giving way to the first sign of blue skies. The room seemed to magically grow lighter.

Clay still held her hands against his chest, but when she slipped out of his grasp he made no attempt to hold on. He let his arms drop to his side. Slowly, casually, she began to massage his neck and shoulders. Her fingertips pressed against the hard, tense muscles, massaging them deftly, feeling the tightness give way after a while. She moved along his back, finding each tense knot, digging the tips of her fingers into them, loosening them.

He shifted his body, stretching out flat on his back. His eyes met hers for the first time. She was still on her knees looking down at him. Never averting her gaze, her fingers skimmed languidly down his chest, lingering on his flat stomach. His warm skin had a luxuriant, velvety feel. She stroked his stomach, enjoying the pulsating feel beneath his flesh.

His dungarees were an obstruction. Shifting her gaze, she bent and unzipped the still damp jeans. He helped her tug them off. His bare skin felt moist, cool. But only for a few minutes. The fire took the chill away, but Laine's warm hands helped more than the blaze to heat his body. He lay still, watching her, drinking in the fabulous sensations her touch ignited over every part of him. And he could see the pleasure and satisfaction in her eyes as she saw the effects of her caresses, her loving strokes.

Pausing, she quickly slipped her sweater over her head, stepped out of her slacks and her underthings. His outstretched arms enfolded her as she lay against him. Clay cupped his palms on her cheeks, flushed by the fire and her passion, and brought her lips to his in a kiss poignantly tender and loving. Their eyes reflected the passion, sadness, understanding, and acceptance that existed for them both, that bound them together and at the same time created the chasm neither of them could bridge. It didn't alter their need or the pain that would inevitably follow.

There was no rage in their lovemaking this time, no battle to fight, nothing to conquer anymore. They touched and kissed unhurriedly, taking infinite pleasure in each sensation. Clay eased Laine onto her back, moved his lips across her fluttering eyelids, over her elegant, high cheekbones, down the slender curve of her long neck. Lingering at her breasts, his mouth took in each nipple in turn, feeling the rush of excitement in his own body as her nipples grew tauter. His tongue circled her firm breasts, delighting in their perfection. Her stomach quivered as his lips planted kisses on her warm, yielding flesh. He could feel her excitement mounting, her back arching as his lips traveled downward.

She let out a half cry, half moan as his mouth sparked more and more fires inside her. Her legs slipped around his waist, her fingers thrust into his dark, tangled hair. She was going to explode. She was certain any moment she would surely burst open like a volcano that was building.

A long, deep sigh filled the air, a sigh born of such sweet ecstasy that tears glistened on Laine's cheeks. Clay lay beside her now, cradling her to him, exultant at the pleasure he had given. Her pliant body fitted against his snugly. She kissed his lips, then pressed her mouth against his neck. When her breathing steadied, her hand drifted down between them. She began to stroke him, lightly at first, then, feeling his passion build, her touches grew more demanding, searching. Her own desire rekindled, she urged him on with whispered words of pleasure as he again explored her soft body, delighting in yet new places that fired her need.

He moved on top of her, initially cautious not to crush her under his weight. But she proved her strength as well as her urgent desire for him, and soon they moved together mindless of everything but their passion and their liberation.

Later, when only burning embers flickered in the fireplace, Clay and Laine sat on the floor side by side, their backs leaning against the couch. Laine's hand rested casually on Clay's thigh, her head on his shoulder.

"I wish things were easy. Once upon a time I thought they were," Laine said, her words filling the still room.

"Nothing that's worth a lot is easy, Laine."

"I care about you so much." In a softer voice, she added, "I cared about Jim so much too."

"I know." He said the words without jealousy, resignation etching his acknowledgment.

"If only I could make you see that I have to write this book. It's a priority that has to precede any other. Oh, Clay, I'm scared to start again, to—to love again. But you keep tugging at my heart, my thoughts, my needs. You give me so much. . . . I'm starting to believe that a very different future than I imagined could exist for us. But first I—"

"I know. First you have to write the book. I hate the idea. What makes it worse, I understand why you have to do it. But I'll be straight with you. The thought of you comparing me with this man you loved so much, thought so wonderful and perfect, well, let's just say it doesn't fill me with confidence. Jim is a formidable foe. I'm not sure I can beat him."

Laine offered no words of reassurance. She still was not sure either.

He studied her features as she looked at the dying embers.

"I've been searching for some answers," he said softly, "and I realize there's only one. You need to write this book and I need to keep my distance until you do."

She shot him a puzzled glance.

He smiled, but there was no warmth in the smile. "I'm no less concerned than you, darling, about feeling pain and anguish. Only a masochist would wish that on himself, and I assure you I am anything but. I always seek to win, but I'm wise enough to know when the cards are stacked against me. I just can't fight a spirit. I don't like thinking about how he was with you, whether I'm pleasing you as much as he—"

Now Laine cut in, an edge to her voice. "That isn't fair, Clay. I'm not the first woman you ever made love to. I'm not obsessive about the others."

"You're not the first woman I've made love to, but you are the first woman I've ever loved. There's a big difference between the two—bigger than even I realized."

"So where does it leave us?" she said, biting her lip.

"I guess we're back on hold. Until you finish this book." Then to himself, he muttered, "And finish with Jim." He reached for his jeans, easily slipping them on now that they had dried. "I never did share well. When I really wanted something I wanted it all. That still goes."

"All or nothing?" Her heart sank. She already knew the answer.

His hand brushed her cheek, his eyes sadly resigned. Her answer was confirmed.

Clay walked over to the window. "The sun's come out."

Laine glanced over to him. "You could have fooled me."

He gave her a wry grin. "Can we declare this one day a holiday from work? Grab these few hours of sun and wrap it up as a special gift to ourselves. I'll take you down to the honkytonk stretch of Virginia Beach and we'll blow my last cent on the penny arcades. Then we'll charge a soft shell crab dinner, devour every succulent bite and then . . ."

Laine, dressed now, stood and walked over to him. "And then?"

He put his arm around her, kissing the tip of her nose. "And then we'll go our separate ways for a little while. I'll always be here for you, darling, but I'm going to stop battling the walls of Jericho. It's too painful. If they tumble, come for me. I love you. Nothing is going to change my feelings. Only my actions are going on hold. A guy's got to protect himself too. You can understand that."

Laine looked from Clay to the beach outside the window. The sand glistened and sparkled as the sun shed its rays in good old southern style. "Jess and I talked yesterday about taking one day at a time." She smiled up at him. "Let's have our day."

Laine ran upstairs and changed into a light cotton sundress in bold red, yellow, and white stripes that better fitted the hot weather. Clay was waiting in the car, having changed even more quickly than she had. He was wearing a pair of white chinos and a soft blue short-sleeved jersey that showed his fabulous eyes as well as his well-defined muscles off to perfection.

That afternoon they were like two little kids having run away from school, out to have one sensational time before they returned and faced their punishment. Effortlessly they pushed aside everything but having fun. They played the old-fashioned games in the penny arcades and the new electronic ones that Laine could hardly figure out before the signs flashed GAME OVER. They ate cotton candy and caramel apples and threaded their way through the crowds along the pier and rested now and then to watch the people passing them. They shared stories of childhood visits to this area and other vacations they had taken; they laughed at the ridiculous souvenirs that had seemed so unbelievably appealing and exciting when they were children. Clay brought a blanket out from the trunk of his car and they sat on the beach after finding a tiny patch of empty space to settle. The noise, the crowds, and all the action were just the medicine for them both at that moment. They eagerly clung to the day's reprieve with mutual intensity.

Watching the sun slowly begin to set, Laine was reminded for the first time that afternoon of the passage of the day. A wave of sadness swept over her. Clay felt it, too, but he was not ready to call it over. He grabbed her hand and pulled her up with him. He folded the blanket and put his arm around her waist.

"Let's track down those crabs," he said firmly.

Laine nodded her agreement, trying to recapture that effusive mood she'd had only minutes earlier. She caught a piece of it, but the whole eluded her grasp.

Sitting on the veranda of a seaside restaurant, they drank tall steins of cool, refreshing beer and nibbled on pretzels while they waited for their dinner. The place was bustling. They'd had to wait almost an hour for a table, but neither of them minded. Again the hectic excitement of their surroundings served to cushion disturbing thoughts. Their meal finally arrived. At the same time a young couple, both glowing with newly acquired tans, were ushered over to a table next to theirs. The twosome locked hands across the table, whispering words only they could hear. The young man moved his chair closer to the smiling woman, who unselfconsciously hugged and kissed him after he'd whispered something directly into her ear.

Clay's eyes met Laine's. He knew they both had watched the affectionate couple with similar wistful thoughts.

This restaurant was the kind of place where no one asked if everything was all right, and when their meal was left uneaten the waitress didn't ask if there was some problem with the food. She swept it away, oblivious to anything but clearing off the table and readying it for the next pair breathing down her neck.

The time for make-believe was over and they drove back to the cottage unable to muster up any small talk and not wanting to speak of things that mattered.

Clay stopped on the porch. Hesitating for a moment, Laine sat down on a wooden swing and Clay stood poised at the railing, looking out toward the sea, listening to the subdued sound of the water in the aftermath of the storm.

"We should drive back to Washington in the morning," Laine said. Clay knew that it would be too stressful and painful to remain alone together at the house.

"Okay." He turned around to face her, resting against the railing. "When will you leave work?"

"I've been getting things together these last few weeks. Another week should tie up the rest of the loose ends." When he said nothing else, she added, "I'll still be in touch with them a great deal. So much of my story revolves around my work there."

Clay nodded. "I guess we better turn in if we're going to get an early start in the morning."

She had wanted to say something else, but as if he had suspected as much and not wanted to hear it, he immediately walked into the house. Laine caught up with him as he started up the stairs. They walked the rest of the way together. He stopped at his own door.

"Good night, Laine. Today was—very special—very beautiful." He drew her to him for a kiss and a brief embrace, and then he pushed her gently away.

"Clay, I'm not only going to need the help of the organization to write this book. I—I wish you would help me too. We've been through so much of this whole incredible experience together." She saw Clay flinch, knowing she was asking a great deal of him. "Oh, Clay, what we've gone through isn't just my personal loss. It goes so far beyond that. We've both worked so hard, fought so often to bring the truth about the horrors of the MIA situation to the government and to the public. Think what this book could do. Maybe it will get enough new interest and enthusiasm going to make the work less frustrating and difficult. Clay," she entreated him as he turned his head away, "you want this horrendous situation settled as much as I do. It's your cause too."

He sighed loudly. "What do you want me to do, Laine? Sit around and hold your hand while you relive your love affair with Jim, hold you as you sob in my arms all over again about his death? That's a part of your book, too, isn't it?"

"I'm asking you to simply work with me on the things you and I have shared. The rest I'll write alone." Her voice was sharp, but she was sensitive to Clay's position and to the difficult bind she was putting him in.

For what felt like a long time she stared him down. Finally his lips curled into a grim smile. "Will there ever be anything I can refuse you?"

"It's not just for me," she reminded him.

"It is just for you, Laine. And because as much as I know I should push you out of my life altogether right now, the thought of not seeing you makes me feel positively ill. Okay, I'll try to help with the part of your book we share. On one condition. I don't want to discuss or read a word about the part of your book I don't share. Jim is between us enough. I don't want to get drawn into all of your memories. And if they prove stronger than I can handle, I won't promise to stick around. I do have to watch out for my own heart. I hope to keep it in one piece, but I'm not entering this thing with untold confidence." He forced a smile. Whatever was going to happen, he had to be in there fighting—no matter what he had told her or himself.

"Your heart happens to mean a lot to me. I care about it staying intact too." Her body stirred with desire. She wished she could spend the night with him, but his look told her he couldn't risk it. His guard was firmly in place.

Laine whispered good night and resignedly walked alone down the hall to her own bedroom.

CHAPTER SEVEN

"Go on, Carrie. Be honest." Laine sat on the living room floor in lotus position. Several half-empty paper cartons with remnants of sweet and sour shrimp, spare ribs, and moo goo gai pan left a cluttered mess on the coffee table. Leaning forward, Laine manipulated her chopsticks with expert skill and served herself a few more pieces of bite-size chicken.

Carrie leaned her back against the couch. A stocky woman, she stretched her rather large legs under the small wood table. "God, I love devouring Chinese food on a rainy day." *Devouring* was the perfect word, considering she had consumed three-quarters of the succulent feast. Groaning, she patted her ample stomach and laughed.

"Why is it that some women manage to keep their girlish figures and others . . ." Carrie smiled good-naturedly at Laine, well aware that her friend was becoming more agitated.

Laine nibbled a piece of chicken and then set her bowl down on the table, the chopsticks tumbling onto the floor. She picked them up and tapped them against her palm. "Are you going to tell me what you think, Carrie Miller, or do I start my Chinese torture?"

"Look, I told you I can't critique on an empty stomach," Carrie said impishly. "We haven't even opened our fortune cookies yet." She looked at her friend and grinned. "Okay, okay. You really want to know what I think?" She pushed herself up to more of a sitting position, pulling her legs from under the table.

"I think it's beautiful. Poignant, exciting, funny. It's first love in all its adolescent bloom."

"Jim and I weren't exactly adolescents when we began dating," Laine said a little defensively. She had completed the first three chapters of her book, offering them only to Carrie for an outside opinion. Now she began to regret having let anyone see it yet.

Carrie gave Laine an understanding smile. "You weren't all grown up either. Besides, if you are going to start getting pouty, I won't shower another word of praise on this sure-to-be best seller."

"You really think it's that good?" Laine forgot her irritation. She hadn't written in such a long time. The experience of taking it up again, this time giving herself what seemed like a monumental task, had been exhilarating. The long hours, hundreds of cups of coffee, callused fingers—she hadn't minded one moment. From the start of the first page she was carried away by the project, lost not so much in the memories as in the excitement of creating a story that was alive and vibrant with interest. There had been a few times, recounting some amusing or romantic episode with Jim, that she had needed to stop for a while, letting the memory wash over her and having to regroup before continuing, but for the most part she felt a joy in sharing the beauty and excitement of falling in love for the first time. And now Carrie was confirming exactly what she had worked so hard to express.

"Of course," Carrie added, her tone more serious, "I know the rest of the story. It's got all the necessary ingredients to make it, Laine. Unfortunately, even the pathos."

Both women sat quietly for a few minutes, deep in their own remembrances. Carrie had met her husband in college too. She and Laine shared that in common. That—and losing their first loves.

"Maybe it was unfair of me to ask you to read it, Carrie. It's got to stir up a lot of old pain for you."

Laine still remembered that awful morning when she learned John Miller was dead. Carrie had been bubbly and in particularly high spirits that day because the organization had just gotten some badly needed funding and the promise of renewed efforts in their cause.

Carrie had always held on to the firm belief

that John was still alive. She had been pregnant when he disappeared only a few months after going overseas. Whether or not it was solely the stress, Carrie suffered a miscarriage a couple of weeks after she had heard the news. Laine had been with her in the hospital all through the painful, tragic ordeal. She still became teary-eyed whenever she thought about Carrie's words to her when she came out of surgery. Weak with exhaustion and despair, she had clung to Laine's hand and said, "I've lost my baby, Laine, but I know now that God will be merciful and spare John. I can't lose them both."

But she had, just as so many other other wives and mothers had lost their loved ones.

Misty-eyed, Laine asked softly, "Does it ever get easier?"

Carrie wiped away a few tears and said, "It's always painful for me when I think about John. But now it's almost like it all happened to someone else. Oh, it's not that I don't still feel it personally. It's difficult to explain. In so many ways I'm a different person than I was when John went off to war. I was barely out of college, starting my first job, pregnant, nervous to be all alone. I had depended on John for everything. He was not only my husband, he was my best friend. In some ways that wasn't a good thing because it kept both of us kind of isolated and insular. Anyway, these past few years I've grown"—she laughed—"and I'm not referring to my added girth. Seriously, I don't think John would believe how independent and competent

I've become, how outgoing and assertive I can be now. I want very different things from life at this point—and different things from love too."

Laine studied her friend with new understanding and admiration. Carrie really had managed not only to come through a personal tragedy with strength and courage; she had grown to be her own woman. Laine found herself hoping she would do even half as well.

"Guess what?" Carrie tossed out the question abruptly, trying unsuccessfully to sound nonchalant.

"What?" Laine was certain this was no casual query.

"I'm getting married again." Carrie flushed, beaming with a wide grin.

"Carrie—that's terrific. To Bill?"

Carrie giggled. "Who else? He's been after me for three months now, and well, I finally said yes. Now it's your turn to be honest with me. Am I doing the right thing?"

"Are you kidding? Oh, Carrie, there's no one in this world who deserves to be happy more than you. And Bill is a great guy. In fact the two of you are a perfect pair. . . ." She hadn't meant to start crying. She was shocked that the sobs were actually coming from her. Her words drowned in her sudden breakdown.

Carrie moved over to Laine, her bulk in no way hampering her movements now. She put her arm around her friend and let her cry it out for a few minutes. Finally, when Laine calmed down some, Carrie said affectionately, "Hey, you're supposed to save your tears for the wedding day, pal. Although it's just as well you get them over with now, since I don't want my maid of honor upstaging me on my big day."

Laine blew her nose into a napkin. "I don't know what came over me. Here I am, ecstatic about your news, and I become positively hysterical."

"Maybe Clay has something to do with your collapse?" Bonnie asked gently, having no doubt that was what it was about. For a while there, she had thought Laine and Clay were really going to make it. She had been on to the two of them long before they had admitted as much to each other, and maybe even to themselves. Lately when Carrie saw Laine and Clay together there was an awkward tension between them that didn't take any great insight to spot. Carrie had brought Clay's name up several times, trying to get Laine to talk about what was happening, but Laine had been adamantly tightlipped about it.

Laine's first impulse was to continue to keep that door closed, but then she looked over at Carrie and sighed.

"He's got everything to do with it." She waited for Carrie to ask more, but Carrie had already decided that Laine needed to make her own decision about whether or not to share her feelings.

Laine picked up the chopsticks again, toyed with them for a minute, and then resolutely stuck them into one of the paper containers.

"I think I'm in love with him, Carrie."

"So, what else is new? And don't tell me he's in love with you. Both of those facts have been givens for ages. Get to the bad part—or do I have to read the rest of your book?"

"I haven't even figured out what to say in those chapters." Laine smiled faintly. "I have no idea how the story is going to end where Clay is concerned. He's furious with me right now."

"Furious?" Carrie had bumped into Clay and Laine only the other day at a local restaurant near headquarters and his big blue eyes glued to Laine appeared anything but angry.

"Oh, he isn't saying it. He's even trying his best to conceal it. But I know just what's flowing through that mind of his. He told me from the first that he hated the idea of my writing this book, more specifically, hating my recounting the time Jim and I were together."

"It's natural for the guy to feel a little threatened."

"I know. It isn't that I don't understand. I'd probably feel the same way if the situation were reversed."

"Well, maybe you need to talk it out, try to help him see why you're doing it. Most important, let him know that writing about Jim doesn't diminish your feelings about him. That is, if that's the case."

"It's exactly the case. The strangest part of writing about the past is that it really is helping me to put things into some perspective. It's like what you said before about looking back with different eyes, as though the past happened to another person. That's how I feel sometimes. Laine Sinclair at twenty was a very different woman from today. Okay—" She suddenly grinned. "Even a drop adolescent on occasion. Twenty felt very grown up at the time, but I see now I had a long way to go."

"So tell Clay."

Laine frowned. "Go try telling Clay Marsh something that he doesn't want to hear. You've seen him in operation. He can be the most stubborn, hard-nosed, infuriating man. All or nothing, he told me a couple of months ago. And as long as I continue with this book—it's nothing, with a capital N."

"I thought he was helping you with this book, collaborating on a large portion of it." Carrie stuck her fingers into the container of now cold shrimp and plucked one out, careful to drop it into her mouth before the sauce dripped on her lap.

"He did agree to help—reluctantly. His reluctance has grown daily. He's playing it so safe and so cool, I feel like screaming half the time we're discussing 'business.' He has made up his mind that I'm using Jim as a barrier between us."

"Are you?"

"No," Laine declared vehemently, and then, "At least I don't think I am. Damn it, Carrie. He is a part of my life. There's no way I can deny that or even want to. He also played a big role in shaping who I am today. I still love him. I always will. And if Clay thinks I can just wipe him out of my heart, well, I guess he's right. We don't stand a chance."

"Listen, Laine, Clay is a smart guy. He's also very sensitive and compassionate. I don't think he wants you to erase Jim from your heart or your mind. He just doesn't want to feel he's in competition with your memories."

"That's exactly what he said. Are the two of you in collusion?"

Carrie chuckled. "Sweetie, I've been through this whole scene with Bill. I think it's probably universal. Jealousy is a natural given in this kind of situation. And let me tell you, I had to do a lot of hard thinking about whether or not John would always bar the way to my making a go of it with Bill. For a long while I wasn't sure. I really had to figure out just where John belonged in the scheme of things. I had to relinquish my hold on him, even on the memories that nurtured me through a very tough time. I'll always love John and I'll have those memories forever. But it's kind of like a scrapbook. You store all your early joys and experiences in it, pore over it hour after hour for a while, then less and less. You keep it always and even take it down from the closet every so often and go through it again, but so many real, current happenings are filling your life that those pages don't hold the same importance or magic anymore. That's when you know it really is the past." Carrie's lips curved. "At least that's how it was for me."

Laine nodded. Carrie had taken something

that felt so overwhelmingly complex to her and translated it into something elegantly simple. Laine suddenly saw that to Clay her writing symbolized a much perused scrapbook. And she still wasn't ready to put it away. The past for her had not yet receded to the place it had for Carrie. Realizing that helped Laine more than anything else to be compassionate to Clay's feelings. She also believed that someday she would be able to stop poring over the book. All she could do was hope Clay would wait.

Laine skirted the crowded restaurant with her eyes, finally spotting Clay. She unbuttoned her burgundy wool coat as she made her way over to him. He was sitting in a corner of the room.

As soon as she came toward the table Clay lifted up his menu. Laine was struck by the gesture, viewing it as a symbolic expression of the walls Clay had erected between them over the past four months. On impulse she took the chair across from him and moved it to his side. A hovering waiter rushed over to shift the place setting for her.

"Boy, it's cold out there. I can't remember an icier November in D.C." She rubbed her hands together before taking the menu from the waiter.

Clay mumbled something and studied the offerings. Outwardly he appeared calm, with that off-hand disinterest that had become more and more irritating to Laine. Had she known the turmoil that was wreaking havoc on his insides, she might have still been upset, but for different reasons.

Ever since they had left Virginia that hot summer morning, Clay had been determined to keep his distance. He helped her with some details for her book as promised, but he went to extreme efforts to maintain a purely business-like involvement. Something had come over him down at the beach during those few days with Laine, something he still had not fully figured out. Hurt. Yes, that was a big part of it. Not just a blow to his ego, but hurt that went deep, deep down. Hurt, like he had never experienced before. He had wanted her so much, so completely. She had become almost an obsession, his feelings for her intensifying despite his vow to stay detached until she was ready to fully give up her love affair with Jim. That was how he saw her writing—as a way to edify and immortalize her love for another man. He couldn't shake his rancor any more than he could shake his love for her. But his feelings about wanting all or nothing hadn't changed either. And "nothing" continued to loom largely in the future.

"Let's see," Laine said, her voice particularly cheerful and animated as she studied the menu. "What looks good?"

Clay glanced up and grinned. "You look like the best thing in the place." She did. Ruddy-cheeked from the cold, that chestnut mane tousled sensually about her face, her eyes bright as saucers; she looked deliciously beautiful and Clay would have loved nothing better than to devour her on the spot. He'd even forgotten for the moment his cardinal rule of detachment. The words had slipped out without forethought.

Laine flushed with pleasure. It was the first time she could remember Clay dropping that damn guard of his in months. It encouraged her to share her news with him now.

"If I look particularly glowing today, I've got good reason," she said gaily.

"Oh?"

"Oh?" she echoed, grimacing. "Is that all you can say? You happen to be sitting here having lunch with a soon-to-be-published author."

She had heard from the editor at McGinn this morning. He had read the first five chapters of her book and he was completely taken with both the story itself and the whole theme, feeling it was just the right timing for a book of this nature to hit the market. A contract was being drawn up, the details of which Laine hadn't even heard. She had been so excited while the editor outlined the specifics that she had nearly jumped out of her seat. It felt like a marvelous, unimaginable dream. Her excitement was still so intense that it took a minute or two to be brought down a few pegs by Clay's forced smile of pleasure.

"That's terrific," he eked out.

"You're damn right it's terrific. You could sound a little happier, if for the fact alone that you had a large hand in it. Steve Fulton, that's the editor I'll be working with at McGinn, is particularly enthusiastic about your input. He thinks it's the real icing on the cake, what makes it so special."

She was hurt, but she was more angry. "I walked in here bubbling over with joy."

"I'm not bursting your bubble, Laine. I told you I think what you've done is quite an accomplishment. I'm—I always thought you were a wonderful writer."

"Good. Then since you are so elated," she said facetiously, "you won't be averse to a little celebration." She said it as though it were a totally spontaneous thought. The truth was she had been thinking about it nonstop ever since her phone call from McGinn this morning.

"Sure. Let's order the best bottle of champagne in the place," he said, looking around for a waiter.

"No," she said so sharply Clay stared at her open-mouthed. "I mean, that's not what I . . . Clay, I want you to come over this evening to my house for dinner. I want a private celebration, just the two of us. I'll make you the best steak this side of Texas, those stuffed baked potatoes you always loved, and your favorite apple pie. We haven't spent a moment alone in . . . in a long time. What do you say?"

Clay's frown said enough.

But this time Laine wasn't going to play into his game of self-defense. The idea had embedded itself in her mind and she was not going to be swayed. They had to spend some time alone together. These past months he had been in her thoughts constantly, filling most of her dreams as well. She had played his game according to his rules, at first because she agreed it made sense and later, when she started feeling it made absolutely no sense at all, she continued playing it out of anger. All these months she had been working through her past, coming to see that a door was beginning to close on that part of her life, and Clay seemed to have spent these months building up his own private barriers. Maybe he was starting to think that his feelings for her weren't as deep as he had believed. Maybe time was giving him second thoughts. Laine was determined to find out where things stood and she was not going to discover any answers in offices or crowded restaurants.

"Why don't I take you out to Antoine's tonight instead? After all, you deserve the very best for your celebration." He could see the suggestion was not going over big.

"It's my celebration and I want to have it my way," she snapped. She sounded like a five-year-old who was going to get what she wanted come hell or high water. Clay laughed, Laine joining in. "What's the matter, Clay? You chicken?" He had used that one on her to get her to agree to go with him to Virginia. Now it was her turn. He couldn't turn down a challenge any more than she could.

Clay gave her one of his pondering, penetrating looks, then leaned over to her and whispered in her ear, "Cluck."

The breathiness went right through her. She

looked up at him with a sensual smile. "Is that a cluck yes or a cluck no?"

"Don't forget to peel the apples."

She had been cool and efficient all afternoon. After taking the pie out of the oven and getting the potatoes set to go in later in the evening, she took a long, leisurely bubble bath, scenting herself afterward with a new lotion she'd spent a fortune on. The exotic scent tickled her nostrils with pleasure and she fully hoped it would have the same effect on Clay.

It wasn't until she went to her closet to decide on what to wear that the tension managed to take hold. She began pulling out one outfit after another, holding each of them in front of her at the full-length mirror, then tossing them one by one on her bed. In record time half her closet was piled on top of the blankets.

This is crazy, she told herself. Any one of the outfits in that pile would have been fine. But not perfect. And Laine wanted something perfect. She finally found exactly what she was looking for stuck in the back of her closet. It was a dress she'd bought last winter for a party, but she'd ended up not wearing it because she'd decided it was too provocative.

The dress had been purchased in a rare spirited mood of self-indulgence that Laine had afterward effectively masked. Now that spirit was very much alive and she slipped the soft, feminine crêpe de chine dress over her shoulders. Saucily ruffled down the bodice, its fiery red color was dazzling. The sheer material criss-crossed the bodice, providing a plunging neckline contrasting enticingly with the demure flounce. Against her silky hair and tawny skin the effect was electrifying. Laine slipped her feet into matching pumps, ran a brush through her hair, and dusted her cheeks with some blusher. The rouge was superfluous; her color was beautifully heightened by the anticipation alone.

She had managed to find Clay's favorite Mozart concerto and put it on the stereo moments before he knocked on the door.

When she opened it, he stood there dumbfounded as he took in every inch of her. He was holding, more accurately clutching, a bottle of Dom Pérignon champagne to his chest. She always looked beautiful to him. Every time he saw her walk into a room he was invariably astonished at how stunning a woman she was. But tonight she took his breath away. It was as though for the first time since he had known her she was deliberately acknowledging her own exquisiteness. Everything about her said, Look at me. I am a dazzling, vital, beautiful woman and I'm not going to try to hide or ignore it anymore. Clay felt such a surge of desire erupt in him that it nearly toppled him.

"Are you going to stand out there all night?" she quipped, perfectly aware of the effect she was having on him, and perfectly thrilled.

He stepped inside, not exactly faltering, but he sure had been steadier on his feet. Laine practically tugged the champagne bottle from his grasp.

"Take your coat off and relax," she said lightly, walking into the kitchen to get some wine. Clay's favorite—Chateau Lafitte, 1978. She praised herself silently for having thought of everything. Returning with the wine, she set it on the table, pouring them each a glass. Clay had managed to get his coat off and was sitting on the couch looking decidedly awkward. He didn't need a blueprint to see the plan at work. Laine, he said to himself, had thought of everything. She was saying something to him about dinner, but his hunger was running in a very different direction. She sat down next to him. Her scent, a spring bouquet of rose and lavender, made his nostrils flare. He leaned over to her and breathed in more deeply.

"You smell good," he told her, smiling. "You look good too."

"I also feel good," Laine said with a provocative wink.

"Just what kind of celebration are you planning?" As if he didn't know. All his own resolves about detachment, keeping up his guard, and all the rest of it, had been left outside her door the minute he'd laid eyes on her tonight. He was only human after all, and he had wanted her nonstop for a painfully, frustratingly long time. Either he was going to have to start recounting baseball averages in his head and get the hell out of there or he was going to have to stay—and celebrate. He looked into her questioning eyes, which looked almost cinnamon-colored as they reflected the vibrant red of her dress, and then slowly, determinedly, he brought her to him. His mouth covered hers and in that instant they both felt connected again at long last.

The red dress lay in a flamelike heap on the floor, Clay's gray flannel slacks beside it. The passion of desire had swept over them with such burning intensity that they cast aside their clothing and any remnants of ambivalence in one fell swoop.

In his arms, the heat of his body against hers, Laine let a small moan escape her lips as waves of ecstasy coursed through her. The first time that night had been frantic and almost desperate, their need overwhelming any attempts to slow down the rising thirst for fulfillment. Now Clay made love to her with less urgency but no less fervor, Laine's caresses equally ardent.

He felt the difference in their lovemaking from those times in Virginia. Just as her appearance had announced a change, her touches, her responses, her commitment, had also changed. Clay felt suddenly scared. Scared he was reading something into what was happening when in truth nothing had really changed. Laine would be more absorbed than ever in her book, its probable success meaning weeks, maybe months, of touring, speaking. Jim would be around for a long time. His hand, which had been resting on her breast, was abruptly lifted.

Laine's eyes sprang open and she looked up at him. "What is it, Clay?"

She had been about to tell him how good he made her feel. She wanted to say she was beginning to put the past in perspective, that Jim need no longer be a spirit between them. Clay's expression changed her mind. He sat up, swinging his legs off the bed, pressing his head into his palms.

"It's no use, Laine. It isn't going to work. I knew it before we made love, but to be honest I wasn't thinking very clearly about anything but my desire for you."

He turned around and faced her. "I read those first chapters you gave me last week."

Clay had not, in all these months, relented about reading the book, but last week she had left a copy of the manuscript with him just in case he changed his mind. She had hoped that by reading it he would realize that she had been dealing with the past in ways that would successfully help her understand her feelings and put them in their proper place. She saw in Clay's troubled gaze that he did not give her work that same interpretation.

In a small, quavery voice, she whispered, "I want things to work out for us, Clay."

He smiled wistfully. "I believe you do, darling. But I don't think you can make it happen. Between every line of that book is the sentiment that's always going to keep us apart. Maybe it wasn't intentional, but by writing this book and seeing it published you have immersed yourself in your memories for years to come. Interviewers, reporters, the public—they'll all want to hear over and over again about the beautiful, poignant details of your love affair. There won't be any way to escape those memories. And I just can't stand on the sidelines trying to pretend it doesn't matter. Trying to satisfy myself with a part of you. When you decided on the book you really made your choice. I knew it then and I'm more painfully convinced of it now."

He got out of bed and dressed quickly. Before he left he turned back to her.

"No more celebrations, okay? For both our sakes."

He shut the door and Laine listened to the echo of his footsteps for a long time.

Her first reaction was anger, but then she admitted to herself that she had no justification for those feelings. In a way he was still sharing her and he had always told her that was untenable. She remembered that night long ago when she had told him that he deserved a woman who could give herself fully to him alone. Clay was right. The book would keep alive memories that prevented her being that woman for him.

CHAPTER EIGHT

"What I'd like to see in that chapter on your initial involvement with the organization is some more detail on the State Department's cooperation or lack of it. Get that Marsh fellow to see if he can dig up some notes or unclassified documents on early briefing sessions. Something to spice things up a bit, you know what I mean. Marsh can be a gold mine of information and you aren't using him as much as you should."

Steve Fulton had the annoying habit of tugging on his ear whenever he made a point. He was tugging away like mad as Laine sat across from him in his executive-size corner office at McGinn. A cold winter storm was in its second day and there seemed to be no sign of a letup. Laine doubted she was going to be able to get back to D.C. for at least a few more days. The thought of being stuck in a hotel in New York didn't appeal to her. She didn't like big cities, only having made her peace with D.C. because of her work and because there was still something southern and distinguished about its urbanity. New York was definitely not the South. She chided herself on being so provincial, deciding with an inner smile that you can take the girl out of the country, but not the country out of the girl.

These thoughts ran through her head while Steve sought to encourage her to use Clay as a collaborator more than she had. Why argue that she didn't need him? She did. And not just for the book. For the past month since their fiasco of a celebration, she had gone out of her way to avoid him and Clay had made no effort to get in touch with her. She was still angry and hurt, the weeks apart offering little in the way of resolve. She had made up her mind that she would write her book without Clay Marsh's assistance. The only problem was, Fulton wasn't buying her changed plan, and she missed Clay no matter how determined she was to get him off her mind.

"I'll see what I can do," Laine said, trying to mask the reluctance in her voice. She was not about to confide in Steve Fulton. He was a good editor, a sharp, bright young man on the way up the publishing ladder. He had taken Laine out to dinner a couple of times, feeling out her possible interest in a social as well as business involvement. Laine hadn't needed to spell out her feelings.

Steve was quick to get the message that Laine saw her contacts with him as strictly work-related and wanted to keep it that way. Steve had too many aspirations and was too smart to let anything personal get in the way of their professional goals. Laine's book, he predicted, was going to be a major best seller. The woman could really write, and the story, part romance and part gritty commentary, was a natural. Now all he needed to do was see to it that she pushed that guy from Special Affairs to come through with some more of the grit. He was puzzled by her reluctance to use Marsh. She didn't impress him as the type who wanted all the glory for herself, and with her knockout looks he was sure she could get any guy to cooperate with very little effort.

"Good, Laine. Speak to Marsh. Tell him the kind of material we want and I'm positive it will put the finishing touch on this whole section of the book." He reached for a sheet of paper. "That leaves the last part of the book. It's still a bit sketchy."

No kidding, Laine agreed silently. The last part of her book was tentatively titled "Starting Over." How Laine Sinclair dealt with her loss, picked up the pieces of her life, and faced the future. For one thing, she was still in the process of figuring all the pieces out and, for another, what she thought she wanted and what seemed possible were two different things altogether. No matter how hard she tried, she could not think about tomorrow without Clay's popping into the picture. She couldn't make it through a single day without wanting him, missing him. Her body cried out for him in the night, all the passion he had unlocked impossible to contain.

On top of being unable to resolve their differences, Clay had begun dating another woman. Laine had run into them once when she was going to a movie with Carrie. Clay and a tall, attractive young blonde were leaving the theater as she and Carrie were going in. They gave each other barely civil nods, both of them immediately stepping up their pace. Another time Laine spotted Clay and the same good-looking woman in a restaurant, but she hurried past, certain Clay hadn't seen her. Even rushing by, Laine hadn't missed the brilliant smile he was bestowing on his date nor the fact that his hand was placed lightly over hers on the table. It hurt so much to see Clay with another woman that Laine couldn't muster any self-inspired words of wisdom or consolation. It also convinced her of something she'd known for a long time. She was in love with Clay. He was the only man she could imagine ever wanting to spend the rest of her life with. She was just as certain that even if he knew how deeply she felt he would never believe she could be fully committed to him.

"Thanks for making this time for me. I know how busy you are." To herself she added, With your beautiful blonde. Jealousy is an ugly emotion, she scolded herself, forcing a winning smile.

"I guess we've both been busy. How's the book coming?" Still safely cocooned with your beautiful memories? Watch it, Marsh, he admonished himself. You're going to keep your cool, remember. Stop thinking about how good she can feel, how fabulously sexy she looks right now. How much you want to grab her in your arms and wipe out all the anger and jealousy with passionate kisses.

"Actually, that's why I'm here." She cleared her throat. No point beating around the bush. Just be straight out. "Clay, to be honest with you, I thought I could, and should, given the circumstances, not hold you to your agreement about collaborating on the book. Well, Fulton, my editor, he's not happy about it. He thinks you have a great deal to offer and so do I, uh, for the book. So I'm here to ask you if you're still willing to . . ." This was a hell of a lot harder than she had imagined. Why did he have to sit there staring at her with such a blank expression?

He was watching the tinge of red flush in her cheeks, reminded of other more intimate times when he'd seen that lovely coloring add to her vibrant beauty. God, he'd missed her. He ached for her and it was nearly killing him to sit there trying to contain himself, keeping his expression blank. It was hard enough coping with his feelings when she wasn't around. Now it was almost impossible. And she was asking him to work with her, which obviously meant spending a lot of time alone together. He wasn't going to be able to handle it.

"I'll offer what I can." He never did listen to his own good advice, especially where Laine was concerned.

"Thanks, Clay." She didn't bother to hide her relief. Nor was she going to try to read any hidden meanings in his words. Briefly she told him the kind of material Fulton wanted and some of her own ideas for what would be of interest.

"Why don't I spend the next couple of days gathering together some info and checking through the records? I'll put my assistant on it as well, and I think we should be able to unearth some early memos and minutes of meetings."

His assistant? Clay never had an assistant while she worked with him. This was obviously a new addition to his staff. Laine couldn't help wondering if the new aide was tall, blond, and gorgeous. She was willing to bet her last nickel that her description was dead on the nose.

"I'm sure if the two of you put your heads together you'll—you'll accomplish plenty." Damn it, she thought, control yourself. In another minute you'll be baring your teeth and really letting him know how resentful and hurt you're feeling. Where's your pride?

She stood up, willing her body out of the archness sweeping over her, relaxed her shoulders, and told Clay she would wait to hear from him.

As she started for the door Clay called her name. She stopped, not wanting to turn around to him. If she did, she might totally forget there was such a thing as pride and go racing into his arms, begging him to forget his damn assistant and everything else but her. But then, wasn't that what he had been asking her to do all that time? It was too late for both of them. She forced herself to turn around.

"I—I hadn't asked how . . . how you were doing. I mean, aside from working on your book."

He had this incredible ability to shift gears midstream. Cool and indifferent one minute, now his whole presence emanated warmth and caring. Laine fought back tears. She loved him so much.

"I—I'm doing fine." I'm doing lousy. I miss you like crazy. I want you so much it's killing me. She lifted her hand to her forehead, brushing away a wayward lock of hair.

"I see you still wear that bracelet." Clay's eyes focused on the heavy-linked silver ID bracelet around Laine's wrist. She'd put it on the day she joined the organization and wore it always, as did so many loved ones of MIA soldiers. Each bracelet bore the name of the missing man and the initials MIA. Symbolic of the terrible situation that still existed, they were supposed to be worn until the MIAs were all accounted for. Laine knew that many people took them off when they learned the fate of the particular man whose name the bracelet bore, but she felt strongly that wearing it afterward acknowledged that the issue was far more than a personal one. She wished she could make Clay see that, but his shield of indifference was firmly back in place.

All she said was, "Some things have changed. Other things haven't." She turned away and left the office. On her way down the hall she spotted a tall, elegantly dressed blonde coming out of one of the other offices. Laine recognized her immediately. Score another one for woman's intuition.

"It's terrific, Clay," Laine said, letting a note of genuine warmth slip into her voice. Her hand rested on the packet of material they had spent the afternoon poring over.

"Of course this is all unclassified stuff and therefore you can use any of it at your discretion. It's too bad so much of what we've been struggling with involves undercover operations that are strictly hush-hush. Hopefully at some point in history it will all come out in the open. But for now, feelings are still ripe with anger, distrust, and downright vindictiveness. And the lengthy list of MIAs is the tragic result."

It had been a long time since Clay had spoken with such impassioned feeling and conviction. Going over the material he had gathered and talking together about many of the operations Clay had headed, Laine was once more reminded of his zeal and earnest efforts in the MIA cause. And Laine knew that there were many undercover operations that would have told even more of Clay's courage and commitment to tracking down the MIAs.

Working together they both were able to relinquish the arch quality to their interactions.

The MIA cause had in truth absorbed them both for many years, that bond still drawing them together as much as it caused their alienation. Sharing their efforts, they were forced to recall all the warmth, support, and caring they had felt for each other on endless occasions over the years. For once Jim was not the focus of their talk and his presence did not fill the room.

Laine stretched. "Now to get this all down for the book. I see some long, sleepless nights ahead of me." She flushed, catching Clay's inquisitive glance. Could he read something deeper into her words? Did he know how many sleepless nights she'd suffered through, not because of her work but because of him? Laine gathered up the pile of papers and swiftly placed them in her attaché case. "I'd better get going. It's past six. Do you have plans for dinner?" It had slipped out. What was she thinking. A nice cozy little dinner in some quiet romantic place and then . . . she was being crazy!

Clay cleared his throat, looking as awkward as she was certain she must.

"Actually, yes. I—I'm meeting someone at seven as a matter of fact. I lost track of the time." There was a blend of embarrassment and impatience in his voice and he pretended a sudden interest in an envelope lying on his desk. He picked it up. A flimsy defense.

Laine studied him pensively. "You mean you have a date." Not a question, a statement.

Clay sighed, meeting her gaze. "Yes. I don't know why I felt the need to be so . . ."

"So circumvented, awkward, embarrassed?"

"Definitely a writer." He grinned. "How comforting never to be at a loss for words."

That wasn't true. Some words didn't come easy at all. "You don't have to feel uncomfortable about seeing another woman. After all, you made it clear more than enough times that you're an all-or-nothing kind of guy. Maybe you've found someone who can give you everything you want." The sarcastic bite of her words came through loud and clear.

Clay came around the desk and started toward her. She wasn't sure exactly what his feelings were or what he planned to do, but she wasn't going to find out. She raised her hand in a futile attempt at stopping him. Then in a pleading voice she said, "Please, Clay. I don't want to fight again and I don't want any more grief. You've been wonderful about giving me this time for my book. Let's leave it at that. You mean a lot to me and I honestly hope you do find what you want."

Clay stood still while she spoke. Then with a slow, determined step he came up to her, cupped his hand under her chin, and kissed her with tender passion. "I hope we both find what we want, Laine," he said, dropping his hand to his side.

She made it out of the office before the trembling started. The sensation moved swiftly in penetrating jets throughout her body. By the time she got home she was exhausted from the exertion of holding herself together.

* * *

For the next two weeks Laine immersed herself in her book, especially in the material Clay had given her. If writing this story had begun as a need to express her feelings and experiences, now it had become her escape from pain and from reality. She worked day and night, every thought forcibly focused on the efforts of the government and private citizen groups to recover information about the MIAs. Carrie, Janet Ross, and other friends saw what she was doing and tried fruitlessly to get Laine to ease up. But Laine turned down invitations to parties, dinners, the theater. She was well aware of what she was doing. But a strong need to protect herself from thoughts about Clay propelled her forward. The book was going well. That was about the only thing that was.

Janet Ross stopped by often on the pretense of asking Laine for some help. She had taken over Laine's position and seemed to have endless questions and concerns about the work. At least that was the impression Janet was trying to create. However, Laine was well aware of how terrifically competent and driven Janet was. She was motivated by the same desperate caring and dedication as Laine had been. Janet's husband was still one of the missing. She and her two teenage boys had last seen him eight years ago. The real purpose of Janet's visits grew out of her caring and concern for Laine. Laine knew this, but chose to use Janet's ploy as hers too. She pretended everything was fine and offered help and advice about the work-related issues Janet invented.

It was a lesson in frustration for both women. Janet had been a kind of surrogate mother to Laine for years, helping her through some rough days and sharing in her hopes and dreams, even as her own despair about the chances for her husband's survival grew dimmer. When Laine was down, Janet kept alive a spirit of optimism and faith and Laine always appreciated Janet's maternal caring and support.

Laine knew that Janet was terribly worried about her, but something kept her from talking about this new, devastating pain that had begun to take root. The truth was Laine didn't want to admit to herself how deeply she felt about Clay, so there was no way to speak about it to anyone else, even someone she felt close to. Janet's heart went out to Laine, but she could not break through the thick shell her young friend had erected. Although she made little headway, Janet continued to pop in every couple of days just to keep the lines of communication open.

Laine appreciated Janet's concern, as she did that of all of her friends, but none of them could fully comprehend the hurt she was so desperately trying to avoid. She could not imagine allowing herself to go through the heartbreak of another loss, so she simply refused to acknowledge the pain that already existed.

The phone call came late one afternoon. The answering machine was on, as it was most days now. Laine wanted no disturbances while she was writing. She had the volume turned up just loud enough to hear the recorded messages and decide whether she should return any calls immediately or put them off. These days she found herself putting them off more and more.

She recognized Clay's voice instantly. It was the first call from him since she'd left his office two weeks ago. Hearing his voice would have thrown her enough, but picking up the blend of distress and anger in his tone shook her to the core. It sounded so familiar—that recorded message all those months ago coming alive again as if it were yesterday. The news that hot summer day had been as terrible as she had suspected, and now she had no doubt he had more sad news to bear. All the recorded voice said was that he would be stopping by after work.

There was no primping this time, no sexy dress, no soft lights, no fine bottle of wine. Laine sat on the sofa in her jeans and a heavy cable-knit sweater, waiting, all her efforts concentrated on keeping herself together. She sprang to open the door on the first ring. Clay gave her a warm smile as he stepped inside. Laine knew the smile didn't come easy.

"More bad news?" She really didn't have to ask the question. Anxiously she waited for Clay to take off his coat and sit down in the armchair. He sank heavily into the cushion and looked up at her.

"Harvey Ross's body was identified yesterday. The news came through a couple of hours ago.

I thought you would want to be the one to break it to Janet." Clay raised his hands, staring blankly at them and let them drop again. "When is it all going to end? I wonder."

Clay had known Harvey from their early years in the government together. Janet had gotten involved with the MIA group through Clay's encouragement. He had been very pleased by the tight bond that had developed between his friend's wife and Laine, feeling that their friendship and mutual support helped both of them through some tough times. No time was tougher for Janet than now, and while Clay grieved personally for the loss of his friend, his heart went out to Janet and the boys, whose dreams and hopes had come to a final end. He looked over at Laine, who had sat down across from him on the couch. She was so still, so poised. He could see the bravery she was trying so hard to muster, calling forth the courage she would need to face Janet with the tragic news.

"I thought we could go together," he said softly. He was pale and felt completely drained. All he wanted to do right now was crawl into a warm bed and try to forget the whole lousy business. But that wasn't in the cards for either of them.

"Yes, I think Janet would want us both there. I—I want you there."

He walked over and took her hands, lifting her to him. She sighed deeply as Clay's strong, comforting arms encircled her. They stood embracing for several minutes, giving each other support and courage. Most importantly they felt that unique sense of sharing that always touched them both so deeply. Now it gave them the strength to cast aside their personal grief and offer Janet what little they could.

It was after midnight when they returned to Laine's apartment. They had sat with Janet and the boys for hours. It wasn't that either Laine or Clay could do anything to assuage the pain, but somehow their presence alone seemed to provide a base of comfort. Mostly Janet and Clay talked about Harvey and the times they had shared together. The boys listened attentively, taking in the talk, knowing it was the only legacy they had. Laine made endless pots of coffee, held Janet's hand when she finally allowed herself to break down, and later sat with her in her bedroom, Janet suddenly looking so young and vulnerable, and so alone. Laine cried too. Sobbing, her guard dissolved, she let Janet hold her to her breast, Janet's hot tears intermingling with Laine's. When they were both cried out, Janet whispered to her, "We're tough cookies, honey. And we're both going to make it. We've had to—for a long time now."

Laine switched on the light in her apartment. Clay walked over to the cupboard and pulled out a bottle of Scotch. He poured them both stiff drinks. Laine took one deep swallow and placed the glass down on the end table. Clay finished his quickly, the stinging fire offering no warmth.

She hadn't taken her coat off. Standing in the middle of her living room, she looked so forlorn and muddled. Clay walked over and undid her buttons, slipping the dark wool coat off her shoulders. He turned, carrying the coat to the closet by the front door. She watched him hang it up. He stood by the door.

"Don't leave, Clay." Her voice was a plaintive whisper. She started toward him. He turned to face her, his eyes intent on hers. When she reached him she stopped, waiting. Never had she needed him or wanted him more. There was no issue of pride here, only of whether he would stay and take her in his arms. Breathlessly she waited for him to make the next move.

Clay knew he should turn away, run out of there. All night long he had been obsessed with wanting Laine, but at the same time as he watched her with Janet, he was convinced Laine's memories of Jim had again surfaced full-force. Was she asking him to stay with her as a substitute? The thought burned in his mind. But her nearness was effectively crowding out everything but his desire and his need for her.

When he bent down and pressed his mouth to hers, Laine gave vent to the feelings that were welling up inside her. She threw her arms around him, returning his kiss with a burning passion. As she felt his hands caress her body she cried out in pleasure and relief.

She was almost weightless in his arms as he carried her into the bedroom. They undressed each other quickly and slipped into bed. Clay pulled the down comforter around them and then pressed Laine to him. She wrapped herself around him instantly, hungry to feel a part of him, holding on for dear life. He was everything she wanted, and she was determined not to let him go. Nothing mattered at that moment but knowing they were one. She urged him on with an almost frantic, desperate need. Clay was swept along by his own passionate longing as well as Laine's.

Even after they were both spent, they clung to each other, neither wanting to risk any hint of separation. Too exhausted to make love again, they still felt the tremor of physical desire pass through them.

She wanted to tell him how much she loved him, but for all the fierce intimacy they'd shared, Clay had been silent about his feelings. Laine fell asleep beside him, her words of love still locked within. Tomorrow, she promised herself before sleep took her off. Tomorrow she would tell him that she loved him. Tomorrow would be the start of a future they would create together.

CHAPTER NINE

It was still dark when Laine woke up. She sensed that he was gone before she even stretched her arm across the empty bed. Awash with sadness and a new sense of loss, Laine grabbed hold of her pillow, crushing it against her, trying in vain to fight the fear, the hurt, the feeling of abandonment.

She had been so certain that they had crossed a momentous chasm last night. Today she was going to tell Clay how much she loved him. She was going to convince him that she could bury the past and start again.

The question burned in her mind. Was last night a sign of Clay still being in love with her, or was it simply a momentary need for solace? She could not ignore the fact that he had been dating another woman. Nor could she forget that she had so pleadingly begged him to stay.

Only later, after the self-recriminations passed, after the hurt and anger at Clay's vanishing was spent did she face the most difficult question. Was she really ready to put aside the past? Could she honestly offer herself completely to Clay? She was willing to fight for him, make him remember how much he'd said he loved her, hold him to his promise to wait until she, too, was ready, but only if she could be absolutely certain she was able to let the past go.

She was ready to start the final section of her book. She was ready to start her life again. And she wanted Clay to be a part of both. But before she could pursue him, there was something she had to do first. For once and for all she had to face her memories head-on and convince herself she was ready at last to bury them.

When the sun came up she had finished packing her overnight case and had called a cab. Fifteen minutes later she boarded the train for Chapel Hill, North Carolina.

Three years ago Laine had come back here for the first and last time since graduation. She had spoken to a crowded assembly of students and professors about the MIAs. It had proved to be her toughest speech. The memories of Jim in this school where they had met and fallen in love nearly undid her. She barely made it through her speech, fleeing the campus and the painful remembrances they provoked. She had never been able to return. Until today.

She stepped onto the platform and removed her jacket. March in North Carolina was much warmer than in D.C. For only a moment she hesitated, questioning whether she should have come. But then she walked with a brisk determined step out into the street.

The college was bustling with activity. The first thought that struck Laine as she stood on a knoll outside the administration building was how young the students looked. Younger than she had looked six years ago, she was certain.

Clusters of people sat on the grass and on the steps to the buildings, while others singly or in pairs and groups made their way in and out of buildings, across the wide lawns and paths; talking, joking, arguing; weighed down with textbooks and notepads, backpacks and bookbags. There was a sense of purpose that filled the air even though a few students here and there lolled around, seemingly oblivious to the busy, intellectual atmosphere.

A young girl jostled Laine as she hurried down the steps. She threw back a quick, casual apology, far more intent on the smiling young man who was calling out to her.

"Hurry up, Pigeon. I'll walk you over to Bergson's class." Jim grabbed her hand and started racing across the lawn. Laine stumbled in the rush and fell onto the ground laughing. She tugged Jim onto the ground.

"Let's cut class," she grinned seductively.

"That's well enough for you to say, my weaver of tall tales, but how am I going to support a struggling young writer if I spend all my time

fooling around?" And then, "Well, there's always another class tomorrow." He gave her his sexiest smile.

Laine blinked her eyes several times as the young couple made their way across campus. She started down the stairs.

Hartford House was the dormitory Laine lived in her first two years. As she walked inside and looked around the downstairs lounge she was amazed at how little it had changed over the years. That same casual disarray prevailed. Chairs propped in front of sofas, girls and an occasional guy stretched out studying, cushions on the floor with more half-reclined bodies poring over books. Quiet conversation going on in different parts of the room.

A diminutive blonde with a frizzy perm manned the switchboard and desk. That had been Laine's job the year she met Jim. He had come into the dorm one stormy day asking to see one of the students.

"I'm sorry," Laine said politely. "Fran Phillips isn't answering her phone. Was she expecting you?"

"Not really. Were you?" He tried to smooth out his tousled wet hair, giving her a sheepish grin all the while.

"Huh?" Not the most profound thing she could have said. She knew Jim Lawrence from her sociology class but only in the most casual way. Not that she wouldn't have liked to know

him better. With those bedroom-blue eyes, blond hair, and lean, sexy good looks it was hard not to feel attracted to him. But as far as Laine knew he had no idea she even existed.

"Did anyone ever tell you, Laine Sinclair, that you have the best pair of legs on campus? Believe me, I've made a careful study of anatomy these past two years at Chapel Hill and you are hands-down the winner."

"What about Fran Miller?"

"Doesn't hold a candle. Her calves lack what her thighs have too much of."

"I mean, do you always throw out compliments to another woman when your girl's stood you up?"

"Who said I was stood up? I found Fran Phillips' notebook and was simply being a good Samaritan. After returning it I planned to ask you to marry me."

"You are crazy."

"Actually I saw Fran drop the book and I concocted this totally ludicrous plot to meet you."

"Why go to such extremes?" She laughed.

"Because I am crazy—about you. Now, don't give me that doubting glance. The first day you walked into class I told myself, Jim, this is the one. Don't blow it. Now look at me. I'm making a complete ass of myself and you probably think . . ."

"I think I've been waiting for this moment since the first day I walked into soc. class. Maybe

we ought to get to know each other—before we get married, that is."

"Excuse me, can I help you?" the frizzy blonde asked politely, turning away from the switchboard.

"Huh—oh, I'm sorry. I must have been daydreaming for a minute. I used to live here in this dorm. I went to Chapel Hill and I was in the area and wanted to stop by, that's all." Laine made her way toward the door as she spoke. "Thanks," she said lamely, and hurried back outside.

Every place she went echoed memories of that long-ago time. She joined the throngs of people rushing into the main cafeteria, extracted some coins from her purse, and bought a cup of coffee and a stale ham sandwich from a vending machine. She found an empty seat. Someone hurrying past jostled her arm, sending the hot coffee careening across the table. She pulled her chair back just in time.

"I love you in brown." Jim grinned.

"Thanks a lot. Next time you decide to get fresh in the cafeteria could you clear off the table first."

"I was only going to wipe off that spot of tomato sauce on your blouse," he said innocently. "Now that you've spilled coffee all over yourself I'll have to take you back to my place and clean you off properly."

* * *

"Sorry, miss. I hope the coffee didn't get you. I'll go buy you another one."

"No, please. I—I really didn't want one anyway. I've got an appointment I'm already late for." Laine reached for her purse and left her uneaten sandwich on the table.

She made her way to the football fields and sat again in the stadium where she had watched Jim in victory and defeat through endless football games. When he won he was like a little boy. He'd whisk her up in his arms, shout and holler, down a couple of mean hot fudge sundaes, and then they'd take a long drive into the hills to be alone together. When he lost it was another thing altogether. He'd stay away from her then, sticking with the team for the evening, going with them to the local hangout where they all drowned their woes in pitchers full of beer.

Laine understood his need for that kind of camaraderie at those times, but she also felt angry at being shut out. Luckily his team didn't often lose, so the issue rarely came up.

Now, sitting on the hard wooden bench gazing out into the empty field, the rich fiber of her life with Jim at the university came into new focus. It had been an enchanting, romantic time filled with all the excitement and vitality of young love. Recapturing those moments helped her to remember just how young they'd really been. Had they been granted the chance to have more time together and the opportunity to experience more of life, Laine believed their love would have blossomed and matured. But fate had stepped in, altering all her plans and dreams of growing older and wiser with Jim Lawrence.

What she could also see now was that during her years alone she had matured. Sure, she would have given anything not to have gone through her painful ordeal. But, terrible as it was, she had learned many things about life and death these past few years. And, she realized, she had learned far more about the depth and meaning of love.

It wasn't Jim who had shared her ups and downs. It was Clay. For so long Clay had stood beside her, giving to her in ways that only now could Laine fully value and understand. His love was not based on youthful fantasies, nor was it set in a make-believe world where the worst catastrophe was a lost football game.

She had treasured Jim all these years, nurturing her hope for his return. But during that same time she had unknowingly been learning what mature love was all about. She remembered what Clay's sister, Jess, had said about a woman in love being very different from a girl in love. Her words sparkled with sudden clarity.

As she walked up a country lane north of the campus Laine did not try to deny or rationalize away her sadness. She was saying good-bye to a happy, carefree period of her life. Saying good-bye to something important was always a little sad. But hand-in-hand with her sense of loss was a feeling of harmony. The battle was over and she had both lost and gained from the experience.

The path led to a lovely old cemetery. In the springtime she and Jim used to walk up here and muse over the old tombstones, fantasizing about the lives of those who lay buried here. Sometimes they'd take their books and sit under the gnarled old chestnut tree, studying together or reading poetry out loud.

"I love you, Pigeon."
"I love you, Jim."

"My first and special love; my sweet, funny, beautiful young love. Rest in peace, my darling Jim."

She bent down beneath their tree and scooped a hollow out of the rich, dark soil. Unclasping the ID bracelet from her wrist, she ran her fingers over Jim's name, brought it to her lips, and then placed the silver in the earthen hollow. Carefully, tenderly, she covered the bracelet with the soil.

She buried many things that afternoon, not the least of which was her grip on the past. Jim would always hold a place in her heart just as she had promised, but she finally accepted that she wanted more from life than memories.

"To everything there is a season and a time for every purpose . . ."

Her step was light and she walked ahead with determination. She finally knew exactly where she was going.

* * *

She called Clay as soon as she got home. His secretary informed her that he would be gone all week—whereabouts unknown. Or not being offered, Laine thought with irritation as she hung up the phone. Now what?

She fought the thought for a couple of hours, but it managed to wheedle its way in at the end. He could have taken the week off to spend it with his—assistant. Laine successfully curbed her impulse to call his office again and ask to speak to the attractive blonde. She had no right to spy on Clay. Besides, she admitted more honestly, if the blonde was also not available, Laine knew she would be devastated.

She showered, took a long time washing her hair, and studied her face in the mirror with unusual scrutiny. Maybe there was some new flaw she could focus on instead of the gnawing insidious worry that kept springing up. Where was he?

She didn't even try working on her book. Flopping down on her bed, she nervously skimmed through a couple of magazines, no article managing to grab her enough to give it more than a cursory glance. Tossing the magazines on the floor, she wandered back into the bathroom, plucked a bottle of nail polish from the cabinet, and painstakingly painted her fingernails and toenails. Surveying her meticulous job, she remembered why she'd never used this polish before. She hated the color. With the same methodical care she removed the garish polish.

She managed to make it through an hour. What felt like an endless week lay before her. She thought about calling Carrie and getting together for one of their feasts, but for one thing, she had totally lost her appetite and for another, the thought of listening to Carrie's wedding plans was just too painful right now. So that idea got vetoed swiftly. She came up with a few other equally unsatisfactory possibilities.

She tried Clay's home phone and hung up without leaving a message on his answering machine. Afterward she fantasized a few apt messages she might have left, even got herself to smile a little at a couple of more graphically colorful ones, but she didn't redial his number.

After checking her own answering machine for a second time on the absurd chance she'd missed a message from him, she gave herself a sound scolding and went out for a walk. Halfway down the block she turned around abruptly, strode back to her apartment, pulled out the phone book, and quickly dialed the number her index finger marked on the page.

"Jess? It's Laine Sinclair."

"Laine, what a nice surprise."

Laine had spoken to Jess only once since that day at the beach house when Clay's sister made the decision to join her husband in Geneva. Jess had called Laine shortly after she had returned from that trip. Things had gone well and Jess felt very grateful to Laine for her support, even though Laine thought she had not done very much. Jess had shown the strength and courage to go after what she wanted. And she had been successful. At least she and David had begun to talk seriously about important issues and Jess was optimistic about their chances of having a more meaningful marriage.

"I was wondering"—Laine tried to keep her voice restrained—"if you've heard from Clay recently. I—I need to reach him, but his secretary says he's out of town for the week. Do you know where he is?" She knew she was fast losing her cool, the frantic note in her tone easily discernible to her own ear.

"Laine, I was just about to fix myself a sandwich. David is at a meeting, the kids are at their grandmother's for the night, and I'd love a bit of company. Come over and raid the icebox with me and we'll talk. I'm not sure where Clay is, but I've got a couple of ideas." Jess's light manner did not camouflage her concern or interest.

Laine consented immediately, promising to be there within the hour. She turned up at Jess's doorstep twenty minutes later.

Jess greeted her warmly and led her into the living room. Cheese, crackers, and raw vegetables were neatly arranged on a platter on the coffee table.

"Wine or something stronger?" Jess asked casually. Then before Laine could respond she said, "You look like you could use something with a little bite. I'll whip you up one of my special martinis. I guarantee it will bring the color back to your cheeks."

"Do I look that bad?" Laine asked with a grimace.

Jess scrutinized her with gentle eyes. "You couldn't look bad if you put all your energy into it. What you look like is an exquisite but miserably forlorn woman who has just lost her best friend."

"That's exactly what I'm afraid has happened." Laine took the cool, clear martini from Jess and stared into it listlessly. She sat down on the sofa and took a sip, making a face at the sharp taste. The second sip went down easier.

Jess joined her on the sofa. She wanted to allay Laine's anxieties, but she was aware she had little to offer.

"Clay called me on Monday. He was supposed to come to dinner tomorrow night and he told me he would have to take a raincheck. I didn't bother to question him about it. Clay rarely tells more than he plans to share in the first place."

"I think he may have gone off with—with this woman who works for him. He's been dating her for several months." Laine bit her lip in an effort not to get teary.

"You mean Denise Sumner?"

"I mean whoever Clay hired as his assistant. I don't know her name. All I know is that she is a stunning blonde and I hate her guts."

Jess laughed. "That's Denise Sumner. Clay isn't with Denise."

"How do you know?"

"Because Denise is probably at this very moment rehearsing for her wedding ceremony. And Clay is not the groom."

Laine sat there, feeling completely baffled.

"Denise is the somewhat flighty daughter of an old friend of the family. She broke off her engagement a couple of months ago, came to Clay, whom she's been infatuated with since she was five, begging for a job; tried to get some rebound action started with my brother, and ended up returning to her fiancé. There it is in a nutshell. Clay did muster a little interest at first, but what he was really trying to do was ease his pain. It didn't take him long to be honest with himself and with Denise. It's you he wants, not Denise, or any other woman, for that matter. My brother is a very tenacious fellow. He loves you, Laine. He spelled it out in just those words when he gave me the news that Denise had quit her job and gone back to Baltimore to get married."

"You don't know what a relief it is to hear all this."

"Oh, yes, I do. The color is back in your cheeks and you've barely touched your martini." Jess chuckled. "Now do you feel up to raiding the icebox with me?"

"You know something. I'm starving. I have a dumb habit of forgetting to eat when I'm all worked up." Laine followed Jess down the hall to the spacious, brightly lit kitchen.

Jess heated up some Mexican chili that her husband had made the night before. The two women finished it off with a shared bag of taco chips and tall glasses of beer. Everything tasted delicious. Only later, over coffee, did Laine start thinking again about where Clay had gone this week. She'd been so ecstatic about the fact that he wasn't off on a romantic tryst, she hadn't given any further thought to his whereabouts. Now the thought not only stirred again in her mind, but she was certain he could be only one place. He had to be on a government mission.

"What's the matter?" Jess spotted Laine's mood change immediately.

"Jess, Clay must be off on some undercover assignment."

"I already figured that out. His voice had that official ring to it that it always has when he's going into action."

"And into danger," Laine added, that forlorn look returning to her eyes.

"Hey, come on," Jess cajoled her. "He's been on hundreds of these things. Most of the time the only danger is in word getting out before some negotiations get finalized. He's probably in Paris or London wining and dining some head of state and doing a little secret wheeling and dealing under the table. You know that's the way dozens of problems get settled. Now, take that gloomy look off your face. I've got some absolutely sinful chocolate ice cream stashed away in the freezer for just this occasion."

Laine made an honest effort to push aside her fears. She forced herself to eat some ice cream but tasted nothing. Outwardly she smiled and chatted, succeeding in doing only a mediocre job of convincing Jess she was not frightened and worried about Clay. Jess let it pass. After all, there was no way to reassure Laine that Clay would be fine. Jess merely clung to an inner belief that it was so.

When Laine returned to her apartment that night the first thing she did was check her answering machine. It was a pointless task. Clay was incognito—unreachable. There would be no word until he returned. If he returned.

She hated dwelling on her fears. Repeating over and over again that Jess was right, that Clay had come through unscathed from dozens of other missions, that many of them were not physically dangerous. But none of her thoughts eased the tension. Could fate hand her another cruel blow? Could she lose him now that she had finally shed the past and was ready to offer herself with an unencumbered commitment? She knew only too well how others had suffered more than once. She fought for optimism against torrents of doubt and fear. And worst of all, she again found herself left to wait—to wait for her love to return.

CHAPTER TEN

She couldn't remember her dreams the next morning, but there must have been something good about them. She awoke feeling considerably better than the night before. Even the chili she had glutted on at Jess's hadn't returned to haunt her. Maybe the bright morning sun—a southern sun, Laine declared silently—also helped. It was Wednesday. Clay was due back at the office on Monday. At least his secretary had told her that much. Chances were he might actually get home over the weekend.

This time when she dialed his number her message came unhesitatingly. "I want to see you very much. Please call me as soon as you get in."

Dressing in a comfortable pair of jeans and a brightly colored red print shirt, she tried to organize the thoughts flashing in her mind. The final chapters of her book were racing through her head and after she quickly swallowed a few gulps of coffee she hurried to her typewriter to get the thoughts down on paper.

STARTING OVER she typed in capital letters. And then her hands began to fly across the keys.

The sharp ring of the telephone disrupted her thoughts. Grumbling, she reached for the phone as she tried to read over the last line she had typed. Then, thinking it could be Clay, she grabbed the receiver and brought it quickly to her ear, the words on the page a complete blur.

"Hello." She could feel her heart lurch.

"It's Jess. I just wanted to make sure you were okay."

"Oh, I'm fine, Jess." Her disappointment was obvious.

"I guess you haven't heard from Clay," Jess said more somberly.

"No. No, I haven't. I left a message for him to call as soon as he gets in. And, Jess, thanks. When I left last night I didn't think your words of comfort were going to do much good, but they did. Maybe I've spent too much time these past few years filled with fear and trepidation. I decided I'm not going to spend this next week doing the same thing. I'm going to use this time to finish my book. When Clay gets back—and he will—I'm going to have completed the manuscript and then I plan to start a whole new chapter—of my life."

"Girl, you are something. No wonder my brother is mad about you. You sound, well, you sound full of life. It's good to hear. I told you all along the two of you have something special together."

"Oh, Jess, the best part is that I feel whole again. I was so afraid for such a long time that I could never weather another loss. Not that I'd ever want to test it out, but I really think that loving means taking risks, even the risk of possible heartbreak. I also see that Clay's as afraid of taking risks as I've been. I'm going to have a battle ahead of me when he gets home. But I plan to fight to the finish and I fully intend to win."

"Something tells me my brother will not be hard to convince. Especially if you come off as strong as you do right now."

"Believe me, Jess, you ain't seen nothin' yet."

"I believe you, Laine." Jess answered with a chuckle, marveling at her friend's recuperative powers. "And I'm rooting for you all the way."

Laine worked straight through lunch. Pausing now and then to reread the fast-growing pile of typed pages, she smiled to herself as she saw the pieces of the jigsaw puzzle finally coming together. This then was the real story—the story of a young woman working through a crisis, coming of age, and learning what it takes to be a woman in love. The words flowed onto the paper with ease now that she had sorted it all out. A feeling of well-being and contentment sprang forth as she wrote. These final chapters did not require any reading between the lines. This love story was written in each word for everyone to see clearly and unquestioningly. The only note of sadness Laine felt was in wishing Clay could be there right at that moment to read the end of her book.

She stretched, her muscles cramped and beginning to ache. Standing up, Laine gathered the pages and made herself comfortable on the couch. It took a good couple of hours to read the whole thing through. Every now and then she grabbed a pencil and made notes or changes. Basically the story unfolded just as she had hoped. All that was left was the ending. And as much as she wanted to finish it and knew exactly what she wanted to say, the closing still depended on Clay.

She had bared her heart and soul and she believed without an inkling of a doubt that she was ready for a future with Clay. The question still remained—was Clay ready? He had wanted her so desperately at first. Had she been able to come through the trauma sooner, maybe things would have worked out more smoothly for her and Clay. But she hadn't, and at least she understood that working through a deeply felt loss takes time and enormous effort. On one level Clay understood this, but time also gave him the opportunity to generate his own doubts and fears. Could she really ever let go of her memories and come to him fully, unconditionally? Laine knew that question tormented him and all she could do was hope she could allay his worries. To do that she had to see him. She quickly pushed aside the terror that she might not see him again.

Janet stopped by around four thirty in the afternoon. Laine must have dozed off on the couch. When she heard the knock on the door she leapt off the sofa as if it were on fire and flung open the door. Again that wave of disappointment erupted as she saw it wasn't Clay. The feeling didn't pass. Janet's edgy manner and obvious worry and tension only escalated Laine's upset. She had been caught off-guard, and her shield of confidence was not in place.

Janet had returned to work a couple of weeks ago. Somehow she had managed to rekindle the same fervor and dedication to the job as she had before learning of her husband's death. Laine admired Janet enormously, remembering how impossible it had been for her to go back. Still she had never regretted her own decision. There were experiences in life you had to let go of.

Janet wanted to talk. Laine suddenly felt a need to postpone the conversation. She was certain Janet needed to tell her something she did not want to hear—something awful.

"Coffee, how about some coffee? I've been writing all day. I forgot all about lunch. How about a sandwich? Coffee and a roast beef sandwich, how does that sound?" Laine was already in the kitchen, shouting the last part, scurrying about, running the water for the coffee, pulling out some bread and meat.

Janet followed her. Her step was heavy. Laine

tried not to notice. She tried not to see the lines of agitation etched on Janet's face. She pretended avid involvement in making the sandwiches even though Janet had not said she wanted anything to eat and even though Laine knew both sandwiches would be left untouched.

Janet gave Laine the time she sorely needed. She sat down at the kitchen table, watching her friend's frantic efforts to gain time and regroup. Laine worked furiously, her back to Janet. And then, as though Janet were watching a movie that had suddenly stopped, freezing the picture frame, she saw the same frozen motion in Laine and heard a sharp cry pierce the awful silence in the room.

"No!" Laine screamed.

Janet rushed over as Laine bent forward, the knife she'd been holding dropping with a loud thud to the floor. For several moments she was oblivious to Janet's words and her touch. Only when Janet gently led her to a chair did Laine come back to life.

"Sit down, honey, and listen to me. We don't know anything yet. The only word we have is that communication has been lost. Several days ago Clay joined a small caucus whose plans were to meet with some exiled Cambodian officials. It was supposed to be a routine undercover operation. With any success we were to get some concrete information about any MIAs that might actually be POWs. I think—and mind you, this is only a guess, as there has been no word—that Clay and a couple of others may have tried some infiltration maneuvers to verify the information these exiles passed to them."

"Infiltration maneuvers? You mean he's somewhere in Cambodia and there's been no word from him?" Laine's voice was a mere whisper and she felt herself shrinking inside.

"Laine, first of all, I want you to promise not to jump to conclusions. Like I said, I'm not even sure Clay went to Cambodia. The information we received, rather surreptitiously at that, since it's still supposed to be hush-hush, is that Clay has not been in touch with the department for the past two days. I gather he was supposed to phone in daily progress reports. His last communication was optimistic. I think he was excited about the information he was getting, but he reported that verification would be essential before any further dealings continued."

"And Clay went to verify it. He would be the one to go. He—he . . ." Laine's voice broke into a sob. "Janet, I thought I'd become so strong. I'm not. I—I can't bare the thought that he's—he's . . ."

"Laine, I told you, no jumping to conclusions. Clay is not dead." Janet grabbed Laine by the shoulders, forcing her to pay attention. "For all we know, he may be on his way home now, or trying to get word through."

"He's missing, damn it. Don't you see? It's all happening again. The not knowing, the awful feeling of not knowing. It's not fair. Do you hear me?" she screamed. "It's not fair." She covered her face with her hands and began to sob. Finally spent, she wiped her cheeks. Her eyes burned; a throbbing pain shot through her head. But she tried to pull herself together.

Janet poured her a cup of coffee and Laine drank it slowly. There was an odd sense of unreality that Laine fought against. She needed her wits about her; she needed to gather all of her strength and courage to see this through. And she needed, most of all, to recapture her faith and optimism. She had to believe Clay would be all right, and she made herself repeat it in her mind over and over until she almost convinced herself.

"I can't just sit here, Janet. Maybe word will come through to you at the office. Could we go there and see?"

Janet had left word that she would be at Laine's, and was to be notified immediately if there was any news, but she understood Laine's need to do something and she readily agreed.

It was well after six when they got to the office. Most of the staff had gone home, but a few people stayed around manning the phones. Minutes after Laine arrived, Carrie swept into the room with a bag filled with coffee and sandwiches. It was going to be a long night. When Carrie put her arms around Laine she could feel the shivers her friend's fragile frame emitted. But Laine held on, refusing to cry and refusing to mourn. There was no reason—yet.

The phone became Laine's enemy. It rang through the night, but there was no word about Clay. A few more bits and pieces of information filtered down from friends in the State Department, but all it boiled down to was that Clay and two other men had boarded a small private jet in Paris for destination unknown. And there had been no word from any of them since that time. It wasn't hard to guess their destination, but the government was acknowledging no involvement with the operation. Laine understood that meant there would also be no overt help for the missing men. They were stranded and would have to make it on their own. And they would. She clung to that belief.

Jess called close to ten that night. She had tried phoning Laine at home for hours and then figured out where she would be. They spoke for a couple of minutes, but had nothing to say. They each held on to two ends of that thin thread of hope, knowing that as each hour passed without word the thread became more tenuous and difficult to grasp.

Laine didn't go home that night. The next morning sheer exhaustion made her take a brief nap on the couch in her old office. Janet and Carrie had taken turns dozing during the night, making sure that one of them was always awake and close to Laine. They were relieved when Laine finally fell asleep, knowing she was going to need as much rest as possible to make it through this wait.

Laine awoke with a start. The silence frightened her and she called out to Janet and Carrie.

Carrie rushed in. "It's okay. We're here. Janet just popped over to Clay's office to see if she could pick up anything more." Carrie spoke soothingly, sitting beside Laine on the couch. She held her hand while she spoke.

"Then there's still no word," Laine said softly. She didn't expect an answer and Carrie said nothing.

"I love him, Carrie," Laine continued. "When you talked about putting away the scrapbook of memories—I can do that now. Oh, Carrie"—her voice broke—"what is going to happen? Am I going to be left with a new scrapbook now?"

"Laine, I wish I knew. I walk around here slamming drawers, cursing the empty air. But there is nothing we can do except see it through and hope for the best. We just can't ever know how many blows in life we'll have to face. But there are also countless blessings and joys. Life is a balance—the good with the bad and all that. How am I doing with my homespun philosophy?" She grinned. "Something tells me you'll feel better with a little food and something to drink. How about it?"

Laine reached up and put her arms around Carrie and kissed her on the cheek.

Time to pull myself together, she thought to herself, and to Carrie she said, "Sound philosophy and a good breakfast are just what I need. Thanks, Carrie. I mean, for everything."

Carrie felt a few tears slip down her cheeks but she smiled broadly. This was one of the blessings she had spoken of—having dear and loving friends. She squeezed Laine's hand as

Laine used her other hand to wipe away some of her own tears.

Laine was surprised at being able to eat. Despite little sleep, she felt rested. After sitting idly in the office while the staff filtered in and began coping with the work of the day, Laine decided to go back home for a few hours.

The phone was ringing as she stepped inside her apartment. It was Carrie. She told Laine to come back to the office. Nothing more. Laine raced back, refusing to let her mind think about the reasons. Carrie met her before she stepped inside the building.

"We're not sure yet, Laine, but someone from the State Department got word to us that Clay's group may have force landed in some godforsaken region of Thailand. Engine trouble. We're waiting for more info."

They rushed upstairs together. Janet was on the phone and shook her head to indicate the call was unrelated to Clay. Laine could not sit still. She began pacing. Every time the phone rang she froze in motion, continuing her step when she knew the call was not about Clay.

Engine trouble, she repeated silently. No word about an actual crash, she comforted herself. A forced landing. Stranded in the wilderness. But they'd been spotted. Maybe even now they were being picked up, flying back home. He had to be all right, she told herself again and again.

"I love you, Clay. I love you." The words echoed in her mind and she willed them to cross the distance and reach Clay. He had to know that she loved him. He had to hear it.

Bruised in the landing, Clay winced as the young Thai soldier bandaged his arm. The other two men and the pilot had suffered a few mild abrasions but basically they were all okay. It had been a miracle. The engine had shut off suddenly and irrevocably over the mountainous stretch in Thailand. The pilot was certain they were all goners and when he began nosing the tip of the plane downward he started saying his prayers. The clearing, a patch no bigger than a postage stamp from the sky, sprang up from nowhere. When the plane finally came to a halt it was almost head to head with a large mountain. The grinding breaks had sent them all flying, but a few inches more and they wouldn't be sitting around able to consider their luck.

Clay had also assumed back up there in the silent sky that it was all over. The only thought he had was for Laine. How could he put her through another loss? He'd attacked her when she'd insisted loving brought pain and now he was going to prove she was right. The pain of what his death would do to her obliterated his own fear.

Boarding the rescue plane, his legs felt rubbery. It was his first realization of how shaken up he really felt and how close he had come to death. His initial feeling was elation that he had come through unhurt and that Laine had been spared more suffering.

During the flight home all of his thoughts were about Laine, about how much he loved her, about the very real risks he would be asking her to face if they tried to make a go of it, about the memories that might still haunt them both. He asked himself if love was always this complicated. He came up with a lot of questions on that journey back home, and a lot of answers. When he landed he realized he hadn't been able to come to any real conclusions.

A typical female response, Laine teased herself afterward. The first thing she'd done after hearing Clay was safe was sit down and cry. Janet and Carrie joined her. They used a whole box of tissues among them. It was a great cry.

"God, I look awful," Laine groaned when she confronted her pale complexion, red eyes, and shiny nose in the mirror.

"I don't think any of us would want to sign up for the Miss Universe contest at this moment," Carrie agreed as she stood behind Laine and studied herself in the same mirror.

"I don't even want to look," Janet concluded, sniffling outside the door.

Laine swung around to face her friends. "Well, I'll tell you something. I may never have looked worse in my life, but I guarantee there has never been a single moment I've felt better."

She called Jess again, having called her earlier with the good news, and she had a second good cry on the phone. Cried out and grinning, Laine proceeded to hug and kiss everyone in the office.

By the time she got home she could barely keep her eyes open. She dropped her blazer on the floor beside her bed, flopped on top of the covers, and slept clear through to the next morning.

That day she waited by her phone again. This time the phone held no terror, but as the morning passed and there was no word from Clay she began to find the steady silence unnerving.

She rationalized that he must have been exhausted when he landed and probably had to suffer through a debriefing as well. She went out and did some errands, testing her answering machine before she left to make sure it was working. When she came back she listened to the few messages. None of them was from Clay.

By that evening she still hadn't heard from him. She finally went to bed. She had a lousy night's sleep.

She called Jess the next morning.

"Have you heard from Clay?" Laine did not try to disguise the angry, hurt tone in her voice.

"He called a few minutes ago. I was just about to call you." Jess did not cover up her agitation.

"What's going on, Jess?"

"Clay asked if he could use the cottage for a few days. He said he needs some time to think things through and decide what he wants to do."

"About me?" The bite in her words showed the concern.

"He didn't spell it out, but that's what I assumed. He said coming so close to dying has forced him to face a lot of things. Don't ask what things—he never does go into specifics. I think he's scared, Laine."

"Scared?"

"Scared for you. He did say that the worst part of the whole experience was thinking what his death would do to you."

"Oh." Laine held on to the receiver, immobile.

"Give him a little time to shake off this mood. Some sea and sunshine always did wonders for him."

Laine mumbled agreement and hung up the phone. For a long while she sat thinking it all over. Many months ago Clay had asked her if she planned to spend her life focused on memories or with a man who could love and cherish her and whom she could give all of her love to in return. In almost losing Clay she had come to see that the risks of loving can be painful but living with only memories would never be a good exchange. Had Clay died, she would have suffered again, more deeply than before, but she would have survived. Like the pigeon, she smiled to herself, she really was a determined survivor and she had learned not only the pain that comes with loving, but the beauty and joy.

The cemetery was empty. A small, solitary, willowy figure made her way along a particular path of graves, stopping at one near the end. She carried a single rose in her hand. Gracefully kneeling before the simple white headstone, she placed her slender hand on the cold granite. She brought her lips to the stone for an instant. Then tenderly, she set the lone red rose in front of the monument and bid her final farewell to Jim Lawrence.

He heard the car pull up. The waves, turbulent during the night's storm, had eased this morning to a low, steady swishing hum. The icy water swirled around his feet. He sensed her presence even though he continued to face out to sea. His heart began pounding more forcefully, but outwardly he remained calm and still.

She spotted the bandage immediately. She hadn't been told that he'd been injured. A dozen feet away she came to a halt. The sea winds made a flapping sound as they hit her thin cotton jacket; the sunlight glinting off the ocean made her squint a bit. She kept brushing the hair away from her cheeks. A lonely ship teetered back and forth out on the horizon, reminding her of a toy boat in a make-believe sea.

Clay was dressed in a short-sleeved shirt and khaki chinos. He looked as he had that weekend last summer, except for the bandage.

She drew closer. Clay remained still, his eyes gazing out to the sea.

She touched his elbow lightly. "Are you all right?"

He looked at her for the first time. The sunlight made her chestnut hair sparkle with strands of gold. He reached over and took a wayward strand between his fingers. She captured his hand and brought it to her cheek. He reveled in the satiny feel of her skin, the mingling of coolness and warmth.

He smiled. "I'm fine." He glanced at the bandage. "It's just a scratch," he added lightly.

She smiled back. "So I see."

"Let's walk a bit," he said.

Laine bent down to unfasten the straps of her sandals and take them off. Then she rolled up the cuffs of her slacks.

He took her hand. They walked in silence along the empty windswept shore, mindless of the cold sea water rhythmically brushing over their feet. As they held hands Laine was filled with the sense of having come home, of belonging. She entwined her fingers with his, Clay's grip tightening in response.

He stopped abruptly and turned to her. Before he could speak, she reached up, placing her hands on his face, and brought his lips to hers. When their mouths touched, all words were cast aside. They kissed, dozens of tiny little kisses and then deeper, fuller, longer ones. And transmitted in those kisses were all the unspoken words, all the love and longing, the joy and pleasure, the delight and intensity of their passion and commitment. They stood against the wind in a fierce embrace that protected them from nature's grasp. They had tempted fate and they had won.

Over and over Clay murmured words of love,

whispering them against her lips as he kissed her.

They sat on the sand, Clay's arm around her as she nestled against his chest. Together they had come to understand and confront their own vulnerability and to realize that it was part of life, not something to try to escape. They faced it now without fear. Finally Clay knew there was no need to fight the past and no way to shed the risks. Where before he had only given lip service to those concepts, now he was able to integrate them into his heart as well as in his mind.

"I'm at the very last page of my book," she said later as the sun was starting to set. "I have an ending." She looked up at him, grateful that his arm stayed around her, relishing the warmth and strength of his body. "But you're the only one who can tell me if it will work."

"What is it?" His hold lightened but he didn't let go of her.

"It goes, 'As she walked along the sand to the man who had come to mean life itself to her, she knew that where memories end, a new love begins.' "

Her eyes glistened with tears, but they were also shining with anticipation. Her love for him filled every fiber of her being. Clay looked deeply into her bright, beautiful face, bent and kissed her eyes, her mouth, the scented spot below her earlobe. He sighed deeply, contentedly, his eyes mirroring her loving gaze. All the doubts and fears had vanished, carried off by the sea, the wind, and the knowledge that their love would see them through all the heartbreak and joy that life held out for them.

He pressed her to him. "It's a perfect ending." He kissed her, his lips trembling against the soft hollow of her throat. "And an even more perfect beginning."

LOOK FOR NEXT MONTH'S CANDLELIGHT ECSTASY ROMANCES®:

266 WINNER TAKES ALL, *Alexis Hill Jordan*
267 A WINNING COMBINATION, *Lori Copeland*
268 A COMPROMISING PASSION, *Nell Kincaid*
269 TAKE MY HAND, *Anna Hudson*
270 HIGH STAKES, *Eleanor Woods*
271 SERENA'S MAGIC, *Heather Graham*
272 DARING ALLIANCE, *Alison Tyler*
273 SCATTERED ROSES, *Jo Calloway*